MAZE

GWEN LINDSTROM MYSTERIES BOOK 2

CONNIE L. BECKETT

ACKNOWLEDGMENTS

Thank you, Donna Russo Morin, for making sure I have my punctuation in the correct places, and any plot holes are fixed. Thank you to both of my writers' groups for their honest critique and helpful advice. We stayed at the Wind River KOA while researching the Dubois area, and both the staff and town residents were helpful with town history and places to visit.

1

MISSED APPOINTMENT

GWEN LINDSTROM POUNDED ON RICHARD STUCKLEY'S FRONT door.

"Richard, are you home?" she shouted, her nose inches from the solid wood panel.

Damnit—she had driven all the way from Dubois, Wyoming, to Casper because the private investigator she had hired said he'd discovered something important about her late husband's missing pension funds, and needed to show her what he had found. Now it appeared Gwen had been stood up. Hell, at eight o'clock on a bright summer morning, was the lazy man still sleeping?

The day had dawned clear and optimistic. It rained in the night, and the fresh scent of warm, damp earth and sagebrush floated in from the car's air conditioner vents as Gwen made the nearly two-hundred-mile drive. When was the last time she had taken a trip outside Dubois? She couldn't recall.

Thirty minutes outside Casper, she had pulled to the shoulder of the highway and called Richard to let him know she was getting close. His phone rang and rang. When his voicemail invited her to leave a message, Gwen hung up. *Probably in the shower.*

She glanced at the dashboard clock. It showed 7:35. A typical time to rise and shower. She'd felt sure that was why he hadn't answered.

Gwen had been so busy at the Ranchers Café—a restaurant she co-owned—the last couple of weeks that she hadn't had time to think about the black hole that was Gabe's lost pension money. June was the height of the tourist season in Wyoming. Visitors coming and going from Yellowstone, Jackson, and the Tetons often found themselves hungry by the time they arrived at the Dubois city limits. She had hired both the young ladies who had interviewed for waitress positions. She'd put Becky on the morning shift, and hired Sandra for the afternoon and evening shifts. They appeared on time with their clothes—jeans and button-down shirts—pressed and neat. Although they were experienced servers, it still took time to show them the nuances of where supplies were kept, and to learn the daily and weekly specials. By Sunday afternoon, Gwen was exhausted and eager for escape.

While Gwen drove, she'd listened to a Dean Koontz book she had downloaded but hadn't had a chance to enjoy. She loved the otherworldly strangeness of his stories.

"No sign of flying saucers yet," she'd said into the car's interior, and smiled.

Gwen had tried to reach Richard a second time when she was ten miles outside of Casper. Again, the phone had just rung and rung, then switched to voicemail. That time, Gwen did leave a message.

"Hi, Richard. Gwen here. Just wanted to let you know I should be there in fifteen minutes or so. Let me know if something has come up."

She'd hoped to hell nothing else had come up. Although the

trip had been pleasant, there were still a thousand other things she could be doing on this Monday, her day off.

"Including fishing," she muttered to herself.

It hadn't taken long for Gwen to find the investigator's house. A late-model Toyota sat in the driveway. After parking on the street, she'd gotten out and headed up the driveway toward his front door. She wondered how old he was and what Richard looked like. She hadn't asked April Erickson, her sister-in-law and sheriff of Fremont County, who had recommended the private detective. His voice had sounded young and competent on the phone. Was he still in the shower, and surprised at her early appointment, would answer the door wrapped in a towel? Would this be a good thing—young and handsome, maybe tousled dark hair? Or would it be a vision she didn't want to be stuck with forever in her memory?

After climbing the porch steps, Gwen had pushed the doorbell. She heard it ring inside, but there was no tapping of footsteps heading toward her.

"Hell!" she exclaimed.

Gwen turned and examined the neighborhood. It was middle class, with crisply mowed yards and clipped bushes. Across the street, red and white rose bushes spilled from a front garden. Somewhere, a dog barked.

Was the Toyota Richard's car, or did it belong to his wife? A girlfriend? A teenage child?

She pressed the doorbell again. Same result: a chime from inside, but no sounds of someone working toward the door. Dammit, he knew she was coming from Dubois. At the least, he should have called her if something had come up. Before she had wasted the day.

She pulled her cell phone from her pocket and called again. No answer.

"Hey, Richard," she said through gritted teeth when his

voicemail came on. "I'm at your front door. Remember, we had an appointment to meet this morning at your house. Call me."

To emphasize the message—and her growing impatience—Gwen pulled the storm door open and pounded on the solid inside door. Still nothing.

"I'm really going to be pissed," she growled, as she stomped back to her car.

Gwen recalled passing a coffee shop before she'd turned into the neighborhood. After turning the car around, she drove there.

One cup of coffee, three fresh doughnut holes, and two unanswered calls later, she returned to Richard's house. The neighborhood was still quiet. The Toyota still parked in the same spot in the driveway.

Before she got out of the car, she opened the visor mirror, ran a comb through her short dark hair, and made sure she didn't have any powdered sugar from the donuts lingering on her face.

She climbed the porch, none too quietly, and rang the doorbell once again. Same non-responsive result. She opened the outside door and dialed his number. Faintly, she heard music—a riff of a guitar. Music had to mean someone was there, right?

She hung up and pounded on the door. Then, after recalling that she had heard that same guitar riff before, back at the Ranchers Café when an alert went off on a customer's phone, she held an ear to the door and pressed redial.

There it was. Somewhere inside the house, music sounded. Odd. Had something happened to him? Maybe he'd had a heart attack. Or had he left in a rush and forgotten to take his phone. In his haste to answer her first knock, had he slipped on a wet bathroom floor, fallen, and been knocked unconscious?

Gwen wished there was a neighbor out. She thought about knocking on nearby doors, but dismissed it. What if her worry was for nothing, and by the time a neighbor followed her over,

Richard was at his door, irritated and embarrassed at what she had done.

She climbed down from the porch and went around the corner of the attached garage. Peering through a window, she saw no second vehicle in the garage, but there were filing cabinets and boxes stacked on one side, and a motorcycle parked in the middle, facing the garage door.

She continued around to the back of the unfenced yard and saw a sliding glass door leading out onto a low deck. *Great!* She could sneak closer and cup her hands against the glass to look inside. Would it be an invasion of privacy? What had been her late mother's saying? *In for a penny, in for a pound.* Tromping through the investigator's backyard and spying into his window was more like being in for a Brinks truck full of money pouches.

"Richard!" she shouted, not wanting to scare a man who was most likely armed. "Mister Stuckley?"

No answer.

Gwen stepped onto the low deck and started toward the sliding door when she saw it was ajar. She saw something… strange. She stepped closer. A smear of some substance muddied the glass. Gwen took two more steps, bent to examine it, and froze.

Light flickered in the room. Gwen's heart leaped to her throat.

"Hey, Richard, it's me, Gwen. Sorry, sorry…"

The rest of the apology died as she realized the flicker came from a muted television. A plump chair sat in front of the television, its back to the door. It was reclined as if someone had fallen asleep in it. The light from the television brightened, and that's when Gwen saw it—a hairy arm in a short-sleeved shirt dangled from the armrest.

"Richard? Mister Stuckley?" she squeaked.

There was a pool of something dark under the edge of the chair. It almost looked like…

"Ah, shit, shit," Gwen whispered in a hoarse tone, and stepped backward.

As she moved, sunlight caught the smear on the door glass, and it shone garnet red.

Gwen fled around the corner and straight toward her car still parked on the street, unmolested in the calm, quiet neighborhood.

2

HELP ARRIVES

THE STREET DIDN'T STAY QUIET LONG AFTER GWEN DIALED 911. Ten minutes after her call, police vehicles whipped around the corner and gunned toward her. She'd been standing at the bottom of the drive near the street, but the urgency of their arrival made her take a few steps back.

Two officers got out, one from each of the two vehicles. They were big, tense, and had their guns drawn, pointed at the ground.

Gwen took another step back and held out her hands.

"Hold on, hold on. I'm the one who called. Better come around back."

She turned to guide them, but a voice behind her commanded Gwen to stay.

"Don't leave," one of the officers said. "We'll need to talk to you."

Gwen started to say, *No problem,* but they had already disappeared around the side of the house.

The day had become too hot to wait in the car. Looking around for a shady spot, she noticed the neighbor across the street had come outside. He was an older man with thin gray hair and baggy pants. No doubt a retiree keeping watch over neighborhood activities.

"Something happen to Richard?" The neighbor strode across the street toward Gwen.

The police vehicles had come without sirens, but their lights still strobed red and blue, reflecting against the man's glasses.

"They're checking," Gwen replied. "I had an appointment scheduled with Mister Stuckley, but he didn't answer the door, so I..."

She left the sentence unfinished, not willing to admit to her trespass, or comment on any assumptions she had about his condition. Richard could still be alive, right? Maybe he was a heavy sleeper, and the stain on the floor was liquor that had spilled when he knocked a glass off in his sleep.

The grim expressions on the cops' faces when they came back dispelled that illusion. One went to his car trunk and pulled out a case.

The other spoke into his cell phone. "We'll need a coroner. Whoever is on duty today." A pause as he listened. "No, we won't need EMS." Another pause. "I'm sure. And the crime scene techs, we'll need them, too."

He turned to where Gwen and the neighbor waited as if noticing them for the first time.

"He's gone, then?" the neighbor said, a tremble in his voice.

The cop gave a curt nod. "Are you family?"

"No, I live over there." The neighbor motioned across the street to his house.

It was the same one Gwen had noticed earlier, with the explosion of roses in the front yard.

"How long have you lived around here?" The cop pointed at Richard's house.

The old man snorted. "I've lived here since my wife and I married back in 1975. Now, Mister Stuckley, Richard, he moved in ten years ago or so. Had a wife, but they're divorced now. He's one of those private detectives. Works from his home."

"And you?" The cop turned to glare at Gwen.

"I live in Dubois. I had an appointment this morning with Richard. I tried to reach him by phone when I got close to town, but he never picked up."

"So you're a client?"

"Yes."

"And you said you just got into town from Dubois?"

"Yes. Well, not *just*. When he didn't answer the door, I left for a few minutes and came back."

Was that a skeptical look on the officer's face? Did they believe she was involved, just because she found Stuckley?

She tried to think of an explanation for tramping around to the back of the house, but every excuse she played out in her mind made her sound guilty.

She shut up.

"The detectives will want to talk to you both. In fact, here they are now."

A car, obviously an unmarked vehicle—the kind with a guard grill in front and multiple antennae—had pulled to the curb as they talked. Both the passenger and driver doors opened. The driver was thick-bodied, and he grunted as he pulled on his jacket. The second detective was female, tall and thin, with a gray sports jacket that looked too warm for the summer day.

The officer who had been speaking to Gwen and the neighbor motioned for them to stay there. He walked over to the two detectives, and Gwen could tell from their body language that he was briefing them on what had happened. After some discussion, the two detectives followed the officers around to the back of the house.

3

———————————

MURDER INDEED

STANDING OUTSIDE RICHARD STUCKLEY'S HOUSE ON THIS HOT summer morning, Gwen wondered what had happened to him? Had he been shot, bludgeoned? Or had he accidentally cut himself with a knife, and then just passed out and bled to death. The sliding door had been ajar, and there was a smear of what she guessed to be blood on the glass. Had Richard fought back, or had he been surprised? Was the scene staged by moving him to the recliner so people would think he'd had a heart attack and died? Of course, there was the obvious dark pool under the edge of the chair. She needed to talk to April, get her input.

"Please come with me," the female detective told Gwen, minutes later, breaking her away from thoughts about calling her sister-in-law, the Fremont County sheriff.

The male part of the team was guiding the neighbor toward his own house.

The detective—T. Anderson, her name tag read—opened the passenger side of the car they had arrived in, and motioned for Gwen to have a seat. At least she wasn't forced to sit in the back seat like a suspect.

Detective Anderson closed the passenger door and went

around to the driver's side. They had kept the car running, and cold air blew from the AC vents. It felt good after standing outside in the heat.

"So was he murdered?" Gwen said first, trying to capture the upper hand in this interrogation.

"Likely."

Gwen slumped. The illusion that this had all been a mistake, and he had simply passed out, dissolved.

"Who would do such a thing?"

"That's what we're trying to find out. Before I continue, I need to read you your rights?"

"What? But I didn't—"

"Just routine." The detective read Gwen her Miranda rights before she could protest further.

April always instructed her to tell what she witnessed, nothing more. But April had also advised that if the interview went hinky—April's word—then Gwen was to declare that she was not talking anymore until she had a chance to consult with an attorney.

After the detective read the Miranda card, and Gwen had agreed she understood it, the detective began.

"You said you had an appointment with the deceased Richard Stuckley?" She turned in her seat to face Gwen and opened a spiral notebook.

Gwen wondered if the car's audio recorder was already chronicling their conversation, as she had seen in cop shows.

"I did. We were supposed to meet at his home when I arrived from Dubois. I was running a little early, so when I was about thirty minutes from Casper, I gave him a call."

"He answered?"

"No. The first time I called, I just hung up, thinking maybe he was in the shower or something. The second time I called, I was closer to town. That time, I did leave a message."

Gwen told Anderson about her efforts to roust the investigator by knocking on his door.

"I have to confess, I was a little pissed by then, after coming all the way from Dubois. So I…" Gwen glanced at the detective, but her expression hadn't changed. "I searched around, thinking maybe he was ignoring me."

That wasn't quite true, but the detective didn't need to know just how angry she had really been about the brush-off.

"A motorcycle was parked in the middle of the garage, so I figured the Toyota was his regular vehicle. Unless, of course, he had a wife or girlfriend. Or whoever used a second one."

She was rambling. Gwen forced herself to slow down.

"So I went around to the back, thinking maybe he had stepped outside to smoke or something. I saw the slider open, and when I looked in, I saw someone in the recliner. Sorry, I trespassed. It's just that…"

The detective shrugged a shoulder. What did that mean? It could be an acknowledgment that they already knew Gwen had trespassed by going around to the back of the house. Or it could mean it didn't matter that she had. The gesture, for sure, would not be heard on any audio.

"That's when I called nine-one-one," Gwen said.

"Did you go inside or touch the back door?"

"No. Oh crap, I did. I cupped my hands around my eyes so I could see inside. I probably touched the glass door with the sides of my hands, but no, not the handle."

"All right." Detective Anderson made a note in the notebook. "Anything else? Did you see anyone in the street? Or a car pull away when you arrived?"

"Not that I can think of. But I'm wondering, how did he die?"

"Won't know that until the coroner is done with the examination."

The detective had other questions: How long had she known

Richard? Had she met with him before? What had she asked him to do?

Gwen answered the best she could, including that the sheriff —she decided not to disclose her and April's relationship unless asked—had recommended the private investigator.

"So the pension money your late husband had was the only thing Stuckley was working on for you?"

"Yes. I'm sure he had other clients, but he wouldn't have told me anything about them."

Anderson paused and studied the notes she had made, before continuing.

"You said he called the meeting because he had found information he wanted to show you. Know what that was?"

"No. I suppose I can't find out about that now, huh?"

"Doubt it. Not sure when we will clear the scene. But regardless, you won't be allowed to go through his house and rummage around for whatever he said he'd show you. That, I do know."

Hell! What had he found? She wished Richard had told her over the phone.

As they talked, a white Suburban backed into the drive behind the Toyota. A young man and a middle-aged woman got out, opened the back, and pulled out a gurney. Watching the activity outside the car, Anderson closed the notebook.

"I'll likely have more questions for you later. I have your number, but are you planning to stay in Casper for a while?"

"Just long enough to grab something to eat, and then I'm headed back to Dubois."

It was a long trip home. Not only had Gwen not learned anything, but she also ran into road construction on the way back. That was, of course, nothing compared to what had happened to Richard Stuckley's day. The poor man. He seemed nice on the phone. The neighbor told Gwen that he and his wife had divorced after they moved in. Gwen wondered if they had children. The thought made her sad, and she drove in silence for a long time, just her thoughts keeping her company.

Thoughts on how she came to be at a dead man's house.

4

LOST FUNDS

IT HAD BEEN LONG PAST THE TIME THAT SHE SHOULD HAVE tackled cleaning out her late husband's personal and business records after he died of cancer. Gwen had carted the storage boxes from the home she had shared with Gabe, to the spare room closet in the cottage where she now resided. The boxes, smelling of dust and old paper, and with their sides bagging from gravity and time, contained the leftovers from Gabe's shortened life.

Gwen hadn't had the heart to go through them six years ago, after his death. She wasn't sure if she could do it, even this much later. Just in case, she'd armed herself with a box of tissues, a mug of strong coffee, and upbeat music playing on the iPod speaker.

"Here goes," Gwen muttered into the empty room.

There were four cardboard boxes in all. She pulled the top one down from the stack and took it to the dining room table. Gabe Lindstrom had owned a construction company when the cancer diagnoses came, which would take him from Gwen and their daughter, Jackie, six months later.

The first box contained the business's old tax records. Most were for years past the time when they would be subject to a tax audit. Before Gwen set them aside for shredding, she skimmed through the projects he had done. The records reflected houses Gabe and his company had constructed or renovated. Some were for places Gwen passed every day on her way to work at the cafe she owned with her partner, Mack. There was documentation on remodeling work: bathroom retiling, kitchen makeovers, and other projects he had done. To her surprise, she discovered Gabe had done the bedroom with an *en suite* bathroom addition for this very house. No wonder she had immediately felt at home when the realtor showed her the property.

The second box contained miscellaneous records that had belonged to Gabe's parents, and that he had acquired after they'd passed. There were journals Gabe's grandfather had written as he emigrated from Sweden. Of course, the writing was in Swedish.

Gwen put them aside, in case a museum might be interested. Then she pulled out a velvet box containing ribbons Gabe's dad had earned while serving in WWII. Looking at records of the Lindstrom family history made Gwen cry. After a while, she went back to her search and found passports, immigration papers, Gabe's school and immunization records, and a small bag containing what looked to be baby teeth. That box, she repacked and put aside to go through more thoroughly.

The third box contained their personal financial records. The old bank account statements, Gwen added to the stack for shredding. Two-thirds of the way down, she found a folder with a label titled *Pension Statements*. Curious. Gabe had been self-employed for the last twelve years of his life.

She pulled out the most recent statement. *Rhett Manufacturing*, the top of the report read.

The name triggered a memory. She had been in her mid-twenties, and Gabe near thirty, when they married. He had worked at Rhett building prefab cabins and houses since graduating from community college. The spring after the date of the last pension statement, they had moved to Dubois, where she bought the Ranchers Café, and Gabe started his new construction company. But that Gabe had a pension account? That had never come up. The young newlyweds had viewed retirement as a far-away, abstract concept.

Reading through the file, Gwen found that at the time Gabe left Rhett, he had accumulated $32,027.47 in his retirement account. That was no small sum back then. And she expected, after years of growth, it would have increased to an even larger amount.

"You always were a saver." Gwen looked heavenward.

The thought made her smile. And then the dashed plans for their post-retirement life made her reach again for the box of tissues.

The annual statements' small print said the pension was insured by the Pension Benefit Guaranty Corporation. What did that mean?

As far as she knew, Gabe never cashed out of the plan. That would have been a windfall she'd remember. Did that mean the money was still available? What happened to a pension if the account holder died prior to retirement age? Did the funds go back into the pension fund pot, or did they go into the deceased employee's estate?

Gwen had no idea all her questions would lead to murder.

5

—————

TRACKING RHETT

THE QUESTIONS HAD FOLLOWED HER TO SLEEP THE NIGHT BEFORE, and as soon as she could, Gwen returned to the folder of pension statements and examined them more closely. The last one was dated in January and covered the previous year's deposits and earnings. The first quarter statement of the following year would have arrived sometime in April. But by then, she and Gabe had moved from Casper to Dubois.

Over $32,000. Why hadn't Gabe sent his old firm a change of address? Or had he? Since she'd always arrive home earlier than Gabe, she typically picked up the mail, but couldn't remember receiving any statements.

Gwen rubbed her temples. The burden of having to once more recall those years of long ago was giving her a headache.

Whatever the reason, no more pension statements had arrived. Gabe was vested. That, she learned from reading the notes on the statements. So what happened to the funds?

She opened the laptop and browsed the Internet for information on Rhett Manufacturing.

Nothing. Which meant they had likely gone out of business,

changed names, or been sold before the then-new World Wide Web could capture the data.

There was a couple she and Gabe had been friends with in Casper: Martin and Brenda Mitchell. They had traded turns hosting backyard barbecues and attended events together. For a while, the couples had maintained contact, even after they moved from Casper. But after Gabe passed, communication had morphed into infrequent telephone conversations and the exchange of Christmas cards with short notes on how the year had gone.

Gwen found an old listing for them in her address book and dialed. It had been years. The last time she could recall talking to her had been just after Martin died, and she had called Brenda with her condolences. Would this still be their number?

"Hello," a voice answered.

"Brenda?"

"Yes, who is this?"

"It's Gwen."

"It's been forever!" Brenda said.

"It has been. I've been reminiscing while going through old boxes from our time in Casper, and I just," Gwen crossed her fingers for the little white lie that would follow, "wondered how you were doing."

They talked for a while, catching up on family and friends.

Then Gwen said, "Didn't Martin work with Gabe at Rhett Manufacturing there in Casper?"

"Sure, sure, I remember," Brenda said.

"The reason I ask is, I came across some old statements for Gabe's pension and wondered what happened to the company."

"They've been gone for a while. Bought out by another firm that later went bankrupt. If I remember right, there was some type of bad management by the new owner, their business fell off, and the company eventually closed."

"I wonder what happens with employee pension funds when a company is bought out or goes under?" Gwen said.

"Beats me. Martin was only with Rhett for a few years. Not long enough to be vested. I wouldn't even know where to start."

They talked for a few more minutes, which gave Gwen time to think.

The very next day, she would contact the accountant she and Mack used for the restaurant business. He might know.

6

TRANSFER LOOP

THE AFTERNOON AFTER GWEN FOUND GABE'S OLD PENSION statements, she called Jack Baker, the CPA they used for the restaurant business.

"How long ago was this?" Jack asked after Gwen explained what she needed.

She calculated: they had lived in Dubois for nine years before Gabe got sick; for three years, she and her daughter, Jackie, had stayed in the house after Gabe died; and then the two years she'd been living in her current home.

"Thirteen or fourteen years ago, at least," she replied.

"Nothing turned up in an Internet search using the company's name?" Jack said.

"Nope. Is there a time limit as to how far back information is collected electronically?"

"Hard to say. A lot of old business records have been converted to electronic format, and can be accessed online. It's just a matter of determining the depository. By that, I mean who is responsible for maintaining or converting the paper records. I'd recommend you start with the Wyoming Secretary of State's Office to search Rhett's incorporation records. Expect you'll be able to do it from a computer. Libraries have registries of companies, too. Was Rhett Manufacturing locally owned, or a chain?"

"They were local, I believe," Gwen said.

"Start with the library. If they don't have anything, give the state library in Cheyenne a call."

Gwen scribbled down the information.

Jack continued. "Company pensions have an administrator who handles the back-office work of the plan. Is there one listed on the pension statements?"

"I recall seeing something like that."

"Good. Try to locate them. Same process. There's also an orphaned pension account database you can search online. Hold on a sec."

Gwen listened to background music and made more notes while she waited.

"Found it," Jack said when he picked up the line again. "Try searching the Pension Benefit Guaranty Corporation database. They keep track of private-sector pension plans if the company goes out of business, or they have lost the account owner."

Gwen wrote down the website address Jack gave her.

"Only other thing is the Wyoming unclaimed property department. If a bank or company has lost track of an accountholder, or a check was never cashed and there's no good address, firms are required to transfer the asset to the state after a certain time. Don't know how that works if it's the company that's lost. It would be your last resort. That help?"

"Yes," Gwen said. "At least, it gives me a direction. Thank you."

"Welcome. Let me know what you find."

———

At the kitchen counter, armed with the list Jack had provided, her cell phone and laptop, Gwen began a search for answers on her own. It wasn't what she wanted to be doing this fine summer day. There were green beans to pick in the garden, and trout flies she wanted to tie. Still, the carrot of extra money dangled. She could buy new tires for her Jeep, or take a vacation in January to someplace with a sandy beach instead of snow underfoot. More importantly, it galled her that Gabe had worked hard and saved to make their future financially sound, and instead of the company tracking him to his new address, the money was moldering somewhere in a lost-and-found department.

Gwen located the website for the Wyoming Secretary of State office, clicked until she came to business entity search, and typed in the name Rhett Manufacturing. The search found the company with a note saying it had been dissolved on December 31, a couple of years after they left for Dubois. There was nothing about the firm that bought out the manufacturing company, but the contact address for Rhett was listed as Matrix Solutions in Wilmington, Delaware. What that meant, Gwen wasn't sure. Would Matrix have Rhett's records?

She did an Internet search for Matrix Solutions in Delaware. There was a company by that name, specializing in management solutions. Those were fuzzy words that encompassed a world of services and didn't help her at all.

As Gwen went to refill her coffee cup, the state of Delaware brought up a recollection. She had taken a business class while at the University of Wyoming. Many businesses, she remembered, were organized in Delaware—that state having the friendliest incorporation laws.

She smiled, also recalling that it was on a visit home to Casper from Laramie, where the university was located, when she met Gabe. He had those rangy, blond looks he had inherited from his Scandinavian ancestors. One look at his teasing blue eyes under bushy brows, and she had been smitten. They had made an unusual couple—she being short with a wiry frame and dark hair and eyes—but their goals and dreams meshed, so their relationship had worked. God, she missed him.

Enough with the pity party. It was time to get back to her search. Gwen went to the web page for the Delaware Secretary of State office and clicked on a link that brought her to the Division of Corporations. There, she searched for Rhett Manufacturing. Like in Wyoming, it listed Matrix as the registered agent, and that the company had been dissolved. Unlike Wyoming, the listing included the Matrix contact information. She punched in the phone number.

"So you're looking for someone to talk to about that company?" a female voice said after Gwen explained what she needed.

"Yes, someone who knows what happened to the Rhett Manufacturing pension plans after the business closed."

"Hold on. I'll transfer you."

Ten minutes later, after many times explaining what she needed, only to be transferred to another person, Gwen had learned nothing. Not only did they not recognize the Rhett name, but they also couldn't tell her anything about how to find out. Privacy laws were the reason they couldn't provide that information, she'd heard again and again.

"Never mind," she snapped when a Matrix employee told her once again in a fake-friendly voice that he would transfer her call.

Gwen got up, stuffed a load of towels into the washer, slammed the door shut, stabbed the appropriate wash buttons, and then, somewhat calmer, went back to the laptop.

The next step was searching Gabe's name in the Wyoming State Treasurer's unclaimed property records. She found the site, clicked links, and came up with Gabe Lindstrom's name. *Oh happy day*. She called the number listed.

A woman answered, and when Gwen explained what she needed, the woman put her on hold.

When the woman came back, she said, "There's a refund from Lander Regional Hospital, and a returned payment from Rhett Manufacturing. One more…looks like it might be an old security deposit return."

"Can you tell me more about the Rhett Manufacturing one? Like, how much the payment was?"

"Since you're not the person identified as the payee, you will first have to fill out a request form, provide documentation showing why you're the appropriate person to claim the funds, if the payee is deceased, and submit it."

"Gabe was my late husband. He had a pension plan that as of the last count was over thirty-two thousand dollars. Is that near the amount?"

"Well, it isn't that much," the clerk hedged.

"Less than $10,000?" prompted Gwen.

"Way less. Sorry, I can't tell you anything more."

"Hell!" Gwen said into empty air, after the call disconnected.

The sun had shifted while she worked, and the garden outside the sliding glass door was now in shade. She would try the Pension Guaranty Company and then pick green beans. That, she knew she could succeed at.

Nothing under Gabe's name when she searched the website. Nothing under Rhett Manufacturing, either. That might make sense if they were bought out and the new company changed the name. She would need to find out if the name, indeed, was changed.

First, the green beans.

7

LOST KITTY

"DOESN'T SOUND LIKE YOUR AFTERNOON WAS MUCH FUN," MACK said to Gwen the next morning, after she explained what she had—and hadn't—found out about Rhett.

He and Gwen stood next to the back counter, having a quick cup of coffee before the Ranchers Café opened at 6:00 a.m.

Mack was the restaurant's chief cook, and Gwen's business partner. He and his family had been imports to the state, having landed here after he retired from the military. That meant that although he was a valuable asset for the business, he did not have a broad knowledge of Wyoming history.

"It wasn't," Gwen replied. "Doesn't help that I'm going back so many years. That was before things were easily found on the web. I'll try the library after work. They might have something."

Lacey, the other morning waitress, arrived. Gwen turned over the open sign, and soon they were busy with customers eager for breakfast and strong coffee.

When business slowed, Lacey and Gwen cleaned tables, wrapped clean eating utensils in napkins, and talked.

Gwen said, "I remember from projects I had to do when I was in high school that there are registries of businesses at the library. You haven't been out of school long. Do you know if libraries still have resources like that?"

Lacey snorted and gave Gwen a wide smile. "You need to go to the library more often."

"What do you mean?"

"I mean, those kinds of databases—the ones for information updated frequently—are online now, accessible through the library website. You do have a library card, right?"

Gwen laughed. "If I have one, it's probably long out of date. That is, if I could even find it." She faced Lacey, her mouth quirked in a smile. "Do *you* have a library card?"

"Yep. Used it just a couple of weeks ago."

A year ago, that would have surprised Gwen. Lacey was in her twenties, with purple strands in her long, dark hair. Tattoos snaked down one arm from shoulder to wrist. Not what you would expect a library patron to look like. But like all the books in the library, you can never judge anyone by their cover.

During the time they'd known each other, especially after Lacey's boyfriend, Donald, was murdered, and she and Lacey had worked together to help figure out who did it, Gwen had come to realize there was far more to Lacey than she first believed. Growing up in foster homes had honed the girl into a self-sufficient, hard-working adult.

More customers came in, and they were busy until late morning. At noon, Martha, the evening manager, arrived to help with the early afternoon crowd.

"You want me to help you search at the library?" Lacey asked Gwen, as they finished their work.

"Let me give it a try on my own first."

"The sheriff might know something, too, since she lived there," Lacey added.

"Good idea. April would have been in middle school when Gabe first went to work at Rhett Manufacturing, but she might remember something like his bosses' names or the company principals. We married while Gabe was still working there," Gwen continued as she and Lacey wiped down tables. "But with newlywed life, being pregnant with Jackie, and my own work, we had better things to talk about than his job."

Lacey waggled her eyebrows at Gwen, who rolled up the cloth and pretended to snap it at Lacey.

"Okay. That, too." Gwen laughed.

On her way to the library, she called April and explained about finding the statements, and her efforts so far to track down the pension money.

"Rhett Manufacturing was bought out after Gabe and I moved to Dubois. Do you remember the name of the company they sold to?"

"Hmmm," April said. "Seems like there were initials. HMR, or something like that. I just don't recall. I was busy with school, and Mom got sick about then. If I remember right, Rhett sold out, but the company that took over didn't stay in business long. Want me to do some checking? I still have contacts in Casper."

"Sure, thanks," Gwen said. "I'm on the way to the library now to check their business databases."

"Good luck." April hung up.

April's guess about the initials was close. At the library, Gwen learned it was RHM Enterprises, Inc. that had bought Rhett Manufacturing. The owners of the new company—just so Gwen's life could become more complicated—had been EC Holdings, LP, and Maritime, Inc. All Gwen could find out, with the librarian's help, was that RHM Enterprises and Maritime were no longer in business, and EC Holdings, a Delaware company, listed Matrix Solutions as their agent for service.

"That," Gwen muttered to herself as she drove home, "completes the endless loop which has gotten me no closer than when I discovered the statements."

———

Thursday morning, she was back at work again, with a headache from the nightmare of the prior day's efforts trying to track down RHM Enterprises, EC Holdings, and Maritime. She had been endlessly transferred from one Secretary of State employee—who knew nothing about the three companies—to another employee who knew even less, other than how to transfer a call.

"I'm about ready to give up," she told Mack and Lacey, as they prepared for the start of business. "Except, damn it, Gabe worked hard for that money, and it ticks me off that nobody knows anything about what happened to RHM's assets or the company's pension plan."

But frustration over her complicated yet unenlightening search wasn't Gwen's only problem that day. Just before she ended her shift at 2:30, Carolyn Hubbard rushed in, red-faced and flustered.

"I'll just take some iced tea, Gwen," she said.

"I'll bring it right over."

Carolyn was a regular customer, in her mid-seventies, and normally calm and well-dressed. Having been widowed young, and childless, she had worked as a realtor for many years, before she retired.

"You okay?" Gwen set down a glass of iced tea and a small bowl of lemon slices.

"Not really." Carolyn swiped at the corner of her eye. "I have this old cat, Callie. Remember me talking about her?"

"Sure I do. Something happen to it?"

"She's missing. I've looked everywhere."

"Cats are pretty smart. I bet she'll find her way home soon."

"I wouldn't be so worried," Carolyn went on, "but she's developed diabetes. I have to give her an insulin shot after she eats breakfast, and again at night. Except, I let Callie out yesterday evening, and she never came back."

This is why I never had a pet. Gwen spent too many hours

working. And when she went home, she didn't want to have to feed and entertain a bored animal.

She said, "You have that field behind your house. You think she might be out there?"

"That's what I thought at first. She likes hunting field mice. That's fine with me. It means fewer of the pests hiding in the garden and invading my house. But I called and called, and I swear, walked every foot of that lot. Nothing."

Lacey had been listening to the conversation. "I'm getting off in a few minutes. I can come by and help you look, if you want."

Carolyn looked at the two of them with such grateful eyes that Gwen found herself, against all logic, offering to help as well.

———

"Here, kitty, kitty," Gwen called.

The three of them—Carolyn, Lacey, and Gwen—searched the vacant lot behind Carolyn's house. The terrain made the search much more difficult. There had been a small cabin on the property at one time, but only crumbling stone walls remained. Add to that all the dead brush and weeds, and there were plenty of places a sneaky cat could hide.

"She doesn't come to *kitty*." Carolyn carefully stepped over the ground. "Try her name."

"Callie, Callie, where are you, little girl," Lacey sang out in that way people, normal in every other manner, spoke to pets.

Gwen stooped to push a clump of sagebrush aside so she could look under it.

"Callie, Allie, supper is on!" Carolyn shouted.

Except for an occasional call-out, the next ten minutes passed quietly.

Lacey headed toward the tree line that bordered the creek

bed at the back of the lot. Carolyn searched along the east side of the lot. Gwen drifted west.

"Callie, supper," Lacey called.

Then she stopped, head tilted toward the trees like she had heard something.

Carolyn stopped searching and watched. Gwen did the same.

Lacey took a few steps toward the trees, stopped, then took a few more. She bent and picked something up from the ground.

Oh God, a dead cat.

And then the bedraggled calico fluff flicked the end of a tail that hung over Lacey's arm.

Carolyn rushed toward Lacey and the fluff ball. Gwen prayed the older woman wouldn't trip as she hurried to join them.

"You gave us quite a scare, Callie." Carolyn gathered the cat up in her arms. "Thank you so much, Lacey."

"Sure. Just glad we found her. She doesn't look real good."

As if confirming the assessment, Callie gave a weak *meow* and rested her head against her owner's chest.

"Blood sugar is probably all out of whack since she hasn't had her insulin for more than a day. I'm going to run her to the vet. Thank you both again so much," Carolyn called over her shoulder, as she hustled Ms. Cat toward her house.

"That turned out better than I hoped," Lacey told Gwen as they headed toward their vehicles.

"Yep."

"I thought when I first saw her lying on the ground that she was a goner."

"She is a fifteen-year-old sick cat. Not sure how much time kitty has left."

Lacey sighed. "I know. Just glad it wasn't on my watch. See you tomorrow morning."

She turned toward her Toyota, parked against the curb.

Gwen stifled a yawn. "See you tomorrow. Thanks for offering to help."

She headed toward her Jeep, parked behind Lacey's car.

There was still enough time left in the day to continue her search for answers on Gabe's pension fund. But first, she would stop and pick up a grilled chicken sandwich for supper. That, plus a side of crisp dill pickle wedges, and some of the tea she made yesterday, would be perfect.

8

FRUITLESS HUNT

After she arrived home and ate, Gwen pulled out the order pad she had used that morning. Earlier, while working her shift, she thought about people she and Gabe had known while still living in Casper.

Of course, there was Brenda Mitchell, who she had called earlier. Some of the people were her pre-Gabe friends from high school and college. Others were Gabe's friends. There were also a few of Gabe's Rhett Manufacturing co-workers they hung out with after work. Gwen had jotted those names on the back of the order pad.

Mark and Lynn Tankerson were the couple she and Gabe saw the most. There was Shirley Hapsen, who had worked in the business office, and had been a longtime Rhett employee. Todd Candon was another of Gabe's work friends on their bowling team.

There were others—co-workers who had come to their wedding, people they used to always run into at the home supply or grocery stores. Some she vaguely remembered, but their names had faded with time and the move to Dubois.

Somewhere tucked in a box was Gwen and Gabe's wedding

registry. She'd need to find the wedding album to help recall those names.

Meanwhile, she would start with the Tankersons. They had traded Christmas cards and phone calls over the years, and their number should still be in her address book.

When Gwen located their listing, she remembered that the Tankersons had moved to Georgia. She dialed Information for their number, trying to recall the last time she had talked to them. The seasons since Gabe died had passed so quickly.

"Hello," a trembling voice answered when Gwen called.

"Is this Lynn Tankerson? This is Gwen, Gabe Lindstrom's widow."

"Oh my goodness. Yes, Gwen."

The voice became stronger as Lynn talked, but it still wasn't the woman's steady speech Gwen remembered.

After catching up on their lives, Gwen explained why she was calling.

"Oh, that," Lynn said. "What a battle. Mark stayed on with the company after RHM bought them out, but things crapped out fast. Rhett was a good company to work for, but RHM pinched the employees until they bled green. First, they cut out overtime pay. Then they cut staff. It was dangerous, as you can imagine. They wanted speed, but when you're building prefab housing, you just can't hurry things. Too many accidents happen with power tools and heavy materials if you're rushed. That's what Mark told me. He had twenty years in and was vested, so he just retired." She snorted. "Although, sixty isn't really retirement age. In fact, he's out golfing today. Hold on a minute."

Over the line, Gwen heard the clink of ice in a glass.

"I'm back. Had to switch ears and take a drink," Lynn said. "Where was I? Oh yeah. Mark was just going to let his retirement account ride with them for a few years until he got another job here in Georgia, but something must have made him uneasy, because he had the account rolled to a broker."

"So he did get his money?" Gwen said.

Another snort. "Finally. But it wasn't easy. The RHM folks kept giving us excuses. They had to make sure Mark was vested, and had completed the proper paperwork way back when he signed up. My man is a paper packrat. He kept everything Rhett gave him—brochures, signed contracts, every statement."

Gwen took notes as Lynn talked, but could barely keep up because the woman spoke so fast.

"Good that he did, too," she continued, "because they kept losing his documentation. My theory is, they purposely delayed payouts until a pensioner finally gave up in frustration."

"But Mark finally did get his money?"

Lynn snorted again. "They eventually asked us to send the originals of any documentation and statements we had. That's when we hired a lawyer. Mark knew if we sent the originals, they would lose those, too. And I'm putting quotes around *lose*, because I suspect anything that came in the door, they just shredded. Must have thought we were hicks out there in Wyoming. Not so dumb we don't recognize a shit pile in the pasture."

She paused. Gwen could hear the sounds of her taking another drink.

"Finally, after more than a year, we received what little was left. That was after they took out fees, taxes, and something they called document research costs. It ended up being about half what it should have been."

Gwen tried to interject, but Lynn just went on with her rant.

Finally, she slowed enough that Gwen had a chance to say, "So all your communications were with the company that bought out Rhett—RHM Enterprises, Inc.?"

A moment of silence over the line.

Then Lynn said, "That was the company Mark worked for

that bought out Rhett, but it wasn't the company we dealt with about his pension. Hold on a minute."

There was the *clunk* of a phone laid on a hard surface, followed a few minutes later by the rustle of paper.

"Here it is," Lynn said. "It took a while to find who we needed to contact. That's a whole other story. We discovered Mark's account was held by WON International. That's capital W-O-N, like they just cashed in the lottery of pension accounts."

"Is WON an acronym?" Gwen said. "Could it be a foreign name?"

"Not sure. Although, *International* could indicate that it was an overseas company."

"Great," Gwen muttered. "It's been hard enough tracking down US companies. How am I ever going to track down one in another country?"

"The letter I have lists an address in Chicago. But when our attorney looked into it, he discovered it wasn't really an office. You know, suite 205 is actually a mail drop that looks legit, but all they do is forward the mail to a different location. So it's possible that WON International is located in a podunk Texas border town, or Hong Kong, or Australia. No way to know for sure."

Gwen ended the call.

This is the point when sane people give up.

Except, this she was doing for Gabe. He's the one who planned for a future he never saw. And dammit, if it meant she was crazy to pursue it, then they could just call her crazy.

It was almost 8:30, and Gwen was fading. Still, she wanted to check one more thing—having ugly suspicions about where a search for WON International would lead.

"Arghh!" she exclaimed a few minutes later.

A computer search of the Delaware Secretary of State's

corporations database had, of course, led her back to Matrix as the agent of record for WON.

"You may have won today," she said into the night, "but this battle isn't over yet."

She was tired. Aggravated. And as she readied herself for bed, Gwen was worried that the nightmare of a never-ending loop of Matrix call transfers would again keep her awake.

It didn't.

9

———

JAY TIME

THE ANTICIPATED NIGHTMARE OF AN ENDLESS MATRIX LOOP became real the next day when, after she got home from work, Gwen again called Matrix, seeking anyone who knew anything about WON International. This time, she would push through the maze of transfers, no matter how long it took.

When the call connected, first an automated voice directed her to push buttons if she wanted to: 1) receive instructions for service of process, 2) their fax number, 3) business hours, or 4) to speak to someone about a company. Gwen pressed four. She was then directed to spell the name of the company on the phone keypad. Damn, she hated this. Painstakingly, she searched the phone number pad and pressed 9 for W, 6 for O, 6 for N. Then 4 for I, 6 again for N, 8 for T.

A voice emanated from the speaker on the phone.

"You're seeking information on WON International?" said a gruff male voice.

Gwen was flustered for a second—*hello, a real live person.*

Then she said, "Yes, I came across the WON International name in connection with a pension plan, and wanted to find information on an account."

Silence.

The gruff voice said, "And?"

"My late husband, Gabe Lindstrom, worked for Rhett Manufacturing in Casper, Wyoming. Actually, I live in Dubois now. I came across some documents showing that Gabe had money in his pension plan. It took me a while, but I think WON might be the holder of his funds."

"Sorry, I can only speak to the account holder," the man said.

Gwen pantomimed pulling her hair out. "Like I said, my husband is *deceased*. I'm the estate executor, and we're tracking down his assets."

True, she had been Gabe's executor. But that had been years ago, and the estate had long closed. Still, it was close enough to the truth, and grumpy Mr. Never-Gave-His-Name didn't need to know different.

"I have probate papers I can send you," she added.

"What did you say his name was?"

"Gabe Lindstrom. I'm Gwen Lindstrom. He left Rhett Manufacturing before they were bought out, but he was vested, and I have papers showing there was over thirty-two thousand dollars in his pension plan when he left."

"Employee funds were disbursed years ago. You're beyond the time limit to make a claim."

Through gritted teeth she said, "Listen, Gabe never received any amount like that. I would have seen it. And," her voice rose in anger, "I handled all of our paperwork. Believe me, I would have recalled a letter like that. You did send a notice informing him the funds were being disbursed, right?"

"Like I said, this matter was closed years ago. Too late now."

"What? You can't just swallow up that kind of money and expect—"

She talked to dead air.

Gwen called back again, this time pressing one to receive instructions for service of process so she could file a lawsuit if necessary. The address was a post office box number. She wondered if it was the same mail drop setup that Lynn had told her about.

Undeterred, she called back again, pressed two, and added their fax number, too.

Gwen got up from the kitchen counter, where she had sat to make the calls, poured a glass of wine, and went outside for a while to sit in the shade and think.

Something wasn't right about the conversation. The first time she had called, no one knew anything about the Rhett companies, and she had been mired in a swamp of transfers. This time, she had pressed the keypad to identify WON, and the man who answered seemed to know a lot about the plan assets. Had he simply been there for a long time, and remembered the so-called disbursement? Was he with WON, or with Matrix? With all the transfers, Gwen had lost track. Plus, wasn't it simply Matrix's responsibility to be an in-state company contact in case they were served with legal papers? Again, the rude man seemed to know more than expected.

Restless, she weeded around the tomato plants. The spring lettuce had gone to seed in the summer heat, and she pulled out the plants, tossing them on the compost pile.

After she went back inside and washed her hands, she called April.

"So you haven't discovered much," April said after Gwen told her what happened.

"Nope. And it really bothers me that they can just suck up employees' hard-earned funds without any notice."

"And you're sure nothing like that came to Gabe?"

"Positive. It's been a while ago, but Gabe hated paperwork, so I handled everything to do with our personal life, as well as the businesses."

"You think they sent it to your old address, and it was returned?"

"That's possible. I know the post office forwards mail for a time, but don't know when that cut-off time is."

"Hmm," April said. "Even if they couldn't contact Gabe, they should have sent the funds to the unclaimed property office if they couldn't locate him."

"I checked there. Nothing that large."

"Let me do some checking on my end. There's a private investigator in Casper that I've talked to before about other cases. Let me call and see if he has any interest. You'd have to pay, but he is competent and quick."

Gwen would call the PI after April got back to her. But first, she had a date with Jay Marker, owner of the local funeral home. Gwen and Gabe had been friends with Jay and his wife, Lauren. Together, the four enjoyed movies, evenings out, and lazy weekend afternoons at each other's houses. After Gabe passed, the visits with Jay and Lauren became infrequent, and then she learned that Jay's wife was diagnosed with Alzheimer's. Failing quickly, Lauren was now confined to a care home, long past recognizing her husband, or anyone else.

Jay and Gwen had drifted closer in their shared grief, and a friendship had blossomed into something more. His wife was still alive—at least physically—so they were respectful. Dubois wasn't a large community. Both of them had social standing as business owners, and neither wanted to fuel the gossip mill.

"I'm surprised it's been so difficult tracking down the funds," Jay told her, after Gwen explained what she had been doing.

They were at Mercer's, a restaurant located on the outskirts of Jackson. Unlike the Ranchers Café, this one was upscale, with white tablecloths, linen napkins, and a great selection of wine. The waiter had taken their order and brought fresh baked bread and salads, along with the drinks.

"Me, too," Gwen replied. "There's an orphaned pension collection agency—Pension Guaranty something. I ran Gabe's name through it, both the old and new company names, and my name, just to see if beneficiaries are listed. Nothing."

"And Matrix is the agent for service of process for all of these loosely related companies?"

"Yes." Gwen broke off another piece of bread.

"Normally, these kinds of companies are just paper shufflers," Jay said, "moving legal documents from one party to the company's actual address."

"That's what I thought, too. But could it be possible that Mr. No-Name once worked for WON International? That would explain why he was so quick to tell me the claims had already been paid?"

"Possibly," Jay agreed.

Gwen took another sip of wine. *Delicious.*

"Enough about that," she said. "How did your week go?"

Jay and Gwen talked while they munched through dinner. Jay told her he had been busy with two funerals. One for a long-time Dubois resident they both knew well.

In all, it was a relaxing evening.

On the way back into town, they stopped at a pullout and watched the moon rise. And a lot of smooching was involved.

Back in Dubois, they pulled up in front of Gwen's house, talked, smooched some more, and then Gwen invited Jay in for the night. A perfect end to the evening.

10

BLACK HOLE

Gwen worked her usual shift at the restaurant Saturday, and then again on Sunday morning. She wanted to start tracking down the company principals at Rhett and RHM, and its owners: EC Holdings, LP, and Maritime, Inc. But work, and the late night with Jay, had worn her out.

Monday morning was Gwen's day off. Refreshed by sleep, strong coffee, two fresh peaches, and the newspaper, she resumed the search. Today, that would begin with another trip to the library.

Before she went down the rabbit holes of EC Holdings, LP, and Maritime, Inc., she wanted to look deeper into Rhett Manufacturing. With the help of her new library card and the computerized library database, she discovered that the company was founded by Hiram Rhett in April 1901. The company initially built wagons and farm equipment. They employed blacksmiths, carpenters, and other craftsmen. In the late 1930s, they dropped wagon building and replaced it with the construction of house kits.

Gwen smiled at this. There were several Sears & Roebuck kit homes in the Dubois area. It had been a great idea—all the parts needed to construct a home shipped as easy as selecting the desired model.

In 1948, Hiram was replaced as owner by Richard Rhett. Must have been a son. Richard pushed the company into the second half of the twentieth century, building prefab homes, vacation cabins, and outbuildings. In 1988, Richard was bought out by McMasters–Bryant, Inc., but they retained the Rhett Manufacturing name. This would have been when Gabe worked for them. Gwen recalled the team of Simon McMasters and Leonard Bryant had been operating the firm up until she and Gabe moved to Dubois.

When Gabe worked there, the company was pulling in a significant annual profit. They paid their workers well, hosted a big picnic in the summer, and a party in December where bonuses were handed out. Of course, they also offered the security of a company pension. She wondered what had happened to make McMasters–Bryant want to sell. Perhaps the two men retired. Or the team had argued and split. Or the company had come onto hard times. Regardless, they had sold out to RHM Enterprises, Inc., and a little over a year later, ceased operation.

Recalling those long-ago events brought up a memory. McMasters–Bryant employed an office assistant who knew as much, if not more, about running the company than the two men did. If an employee or vendor had a question, she knew the answer. What was her name? Karen? No, it was Katherine. No one dared to call her Kathy. Her last name was…

Gwen got up from the terminal she was using in the library. She stretched, the vertebra in her spine cracking as she twisted left and right. She checked out of the computer terminal, shouldered the backpack she used in lieu of a purse, and went to find a bathroom. Sitting in the stall, she suddenly snapped her fingers. Saunders, that was the last name of the executive assistant. The woman had only been a few years older than

Gwen. She wished she knew if Saunders was Katherine's married name or her maiden name.

Back at the computer, Gwen's stomach growled, reminding her it was afternoon. She ignored it and pushed on.

First, she had to find Katherine Saunders. Gwen signed on and checked the Casper area phone directories for the past three years.

Nothing.

She did an Internet search, narrowing it so it would only bring up persons with a Wyoming connection. There were lots of Saunders with the names Katherine, Kathy, or K. Slowly, Gwen went through the list. No Saunders that Gwen could link with Casper during that time period.

She sat there for a minute, rubbing her temples. Then she gathered up her notes, signed out, and went to sit outside in a shaded area of the library. There, she called Lynn Tankerson again.

Lynn laughed when she answered the phone. "This has to be some kind of record. I don't hear from you in years, and then you call twice in one week."

Gwen explained she was tracking down company principals, and recalled the name of McMasters–Bryant's assistant.

"Katherine Saunders. Sure, I remember her," Lynn said. "Now Shirley Hepsan was the human resources manager. Katherine, she was the executive assistant to McMasters and Bryant while they were the president and CEO of the company."

"Do you know if she's still living in Casper? I tried to find her, but she isn't in the phone directory."

"Katherine was terminated shortly after RHM Enterprises bought out Rhett. The new firm brought in their own staff. Too bad they let her go. Katherine was an encyclopedia of knowledge about company operations and the pre-built construction business. She had a Rolodex full of contacts. and knowing her, she left with the Rolodex and job prospects in hand."

"She went to work for another business in Casper?" Gwen said.

"No, I believe she moved to Cheyenne and found a job in government. My guess is one of her old contacts proved useful. Someone told me she was working for the governor's office, but I don't know that for certain."

"That's helpful," Gwen said. "Anything else you remembered after we last talked?"

"No. Just still surprised the company went under. Either someone didn't know what the hell the business was all about, or, in some way, they sucked the life out of it."

Gwen thanked Lynn, and both made promises to keep in touch.

Back at home, Gwen made a ham and cheese sandwich and took it outside, along with a glass of iced tea and her laptop, and sat on the porch. First, she ate. She was so hungry, her stomach would have revolted if she didn't feed it. And then she powered up the laptop and found the Wyoming state government site. Painstakingly, she looked through staff lists of the different agencies until she found a K. Saunders. Katherine—Gwen bet that even now, no one called her Kathy—was the office manager with the Wyoming Oil and Gas Conservation Commission.

"Katherine Saunders, how may I help you," a crisp voice answered when Gwen called and asked to be transferred to her.

"Are you the Katherine Saunders who once worked for Rhett Manufacturing?"

"The same," the woman replied, a note of wariness in her voice.

"My name is Gwen Lindstrom. My late husband, Gabe, worked for Rhett Manufacturing. The reason I'm calling is that I came across some old papers saying Gabe had a pension at the company."

Silence.

Gwen continued. "The statements I found said his account

was valued at over thirty-two thousand dollars when he left. My husband didn't cash it out, and I know he never received a letter or statement after RHM took over."

"I'm not sure—"

"Listen, Gabe died a few years ago from cancer. He had set up an account for our retirement—one he will never have a chance to experience. I've tried everything to find out what happened. I'm guessing he's not the only employee this happened to, but I can't find anything about the pension fund or RHM's principals. You worked for the company executives. Surely you know—"

"Sorry, Missus Lindstrom. I can't tell you anything more than that I worked there."

"You can't, or you won't?" Gwen snapped.

"I can't. I signed a confidentiality agreement. Even if I knew something, I couldn't tell you."

"A what?"

"As part of the settlement. I have to go."

"Wait, what? A confidentiality agreement. Why?"

Dead air.

What in the hell was going on? Why was a confidentiality agreement in play? If Saunders had been terminated, it would make sense that they would reach some type of compensation settlement with her. But insisting that it be kept confidential didn't seem right. Saunders must have received a significant amount of money. Maybe RHM didn't want other employees to know they had paid off their key office staff. More likely, they bought Saunders's silence. Was it because shady dealings were going on, and they didn't want anyone to know? If so, Saunders was certainly in a position to figure out what was happening behind the scenes.

And there was still the question of what had happened with a well-established, profitable company to make it go bust. Wyoming was experiencing a housing boom at that time. Especially since the well-to-do had discovered the area's natural wonders and the fine ski slopes of Jackson Hole.

Gwen's frustration reached new heights. It seemed every lead on RHM led to a black hole of nothingness. *Damn.*

It was time to stop and enjoy what was left of her day.

11

PI STUCKLEY

SOMEWHERE, GWEN HAD READ THAT TUESDAY WAS THE MOST productive day of the business work week. Mondays were… well, Mondays. Wednesdays were the crest of the hill that led down the slope to the weekend. But since Gwen took Mondays off, that meant today—Tuesday—was actually her Monday. The question was, would her quest for information finally be productive today.

The tables at the Ranchers Cafe were filled by seven, and she and Lacey kept busy refilling coffee cups, delivering plates of pancakes, bacon, and eggs, and clearing away the remains of breakfast.

"How's it going?" April asked, sliding onto one of the counter stools near Gwen.

The sheriff was dressed in her usual pressed uniform, and her blonde hair was caught up in a bun at the nape of her neck. She had on a thick belt with all the accouterments of law enforcement: pistol, handcuffs, and a loop holding a heavy flashlight. On a normal woman, this might have bogged her down, but April was close to six-feet tall, with strong bones and graceful movements. Despite her height and weight, though, there was no masking her femininity.

"Doing all right," Gwen replied. "What about you? Things must be slow if you have time for breakfast."

"Just coffee. We're meeting this morning with the city accountant about the department's budget." She grimaced. "And I need fortification."

"Coming up." Gwen grinned.

A minute later, she set a cup down on the counter.

"How are Rod and the kids doing?"

Her sister-in-law had a husband and three sons—teen and pre-teen.

"The usual," April replied. "They come home from summer camp and suck everything edible out of the fridge and cupboards. I need to buy one of those gigantic fridges. You know the ones. Maybe then I can buy enough milk so there's some left for my cereal in the morning." She took a sip of the coffee. "How are things going with your search for answers about Gabe's pension money?"

"It's been like chasing rats through a maze. I think I'm getting somewhere, but I keep running into deadends." Gwen held up a finger. "Hold on. I'll be back in a sec."

She grabbed plates of food off the counter in the cut-through space between the kitchen and seating area, and took them to a table of retirees who met there on a regular basis. Then she took orders for a couple who had come in. One more round refilling coffee cups, and she went back to April.

"I'm good," April said when Gwen motioned at her cup with the coffee carafe.

"Like I was saying. I can't find anything about RHM, the company that took over Rhett. And here's something weird—I tracked down the former executive secretary for the owners, and she said she couldn't tell me anything because," Gwen made air quotes, "she signed a confidentiality agreement."

"Odd. I've seen employment agreements prohibiting disclosure of trade or product information, but rarely confidentiality agreements for administrative staff. Any idea why?"

"She said something about there being a settlement. My guess is she was compensated, a lot, for being terminated. Maybe the company didn't want it to get out that there was money for the asking."

April shrugged. "Or they were buying her silence on something shady they were doing. Who knows. Anyway, one reason I came in is to see if you still want the name of the private investigator."

"I do," Gwen replied.

One of the diners caught her eye and pantomimed writing.

"Just a minute. I need to give a customer his ticket."

"You go ahead," April said. "I need to scoot. Here's his card. I'll let you know if I hear anything. You do the same." She stood and tucked a five-dollar bill and a business card under the saucer.

"Thanks, April."

Gwen went to collect the customer's money.

———

First thing Gwen did when she got home after work was call the private investigator April had recommended. The name on the card was Richard Stuckley, PI. When Stuckley answered the phone, Gwen explained who she was, and that April had referred her.

"Sure, sure. I talked to the sheriff late last week. She mentioned you might be calling. She's your sister-in-law, right?"

"Yes. My late husband's younger sister."

"She told me that her brother. Gabe—is that right?

"Yes."

"Was employed with Rhett Manufacturing, and you recently came across an old pension statement."

"Yes, on both counts. I handled all our personal, and his business, affairs. Believe me, I would have remembered receiving an extra thirty-two thousand dollars."

"And you don't remember receiving any kind of notice letter from the company that bought out Rhett?"

"No."

Gwen explained that the Delaware Division of Corporations had Matrix listed as resident agent for all the companies associated with Rhett, RHM, and WON International and the problems she had tracking down the principals, as well as what she had been told when finally connected to someone.

"Hmm," Richard mused. "You say the man told you all the funds had already been disbursed? Do you recall his name?"

"He never told me his name. But yes, that is what he told me. Do you want the phone number I called? It wasn't his direct number. I was transferred several times."

"Sure."

Gwen gave him the number.

Stuckley said, "The phone number will get me started, but I have other avenues to pursue for information."

They talked for a while longer. Gwen gave him information she had discovered on the two companies that were listed as principals for RHM; told him what she had learned from Lynn Tankerson; and revealed what the secretary, Katherine Saunders, had told her about the confidentiality agreement.

"Let me see what I can do," Richard said. "If you'll give me your email address, I'll send you my standard contract. I can get started tomorrow, but I will need the contract signed and returned. I also require a thousand-dollar retainer. Normally I charge a hundred dollars an hour, but I've had a good working relationship with the sheriff on a few cases, so I'll only charge you sixty. I can take a check or credit card for the retainer. Any unused money will, of course, be returned."

A thousand dollars seemed like a lot. But hopefully he would have better luck than she'd had.

Gwen gave him her credit card information, and he said he would get back to her within a few days.

"I hope this works out," she muttered, as she tucked the credit card back into her billfold.

A THREAT

On the Wednesday after she hired Richard Stuckley, Gwen stayed after her shift to do paperwork. They were still shorthanded in the evening, and she emailed a help-wanted ad to the local newspaper. Next, she typed up a flyer with the same information and taped it to the restaurant's front door. Done with the paperwork, she helped herself to a salad and the spaghetti and meatballs that were the day's special, and took it home to eat.

Perhaps Gwen was looking at the problem wrong. She had been tracking the company as it changed ownership. Her accountant, however, told her that a plan administrator would have handled the pension assets. Lynn told Gwen that WON International was the company they had worked with to cash out Mark's pension account, so it made sense that they were the plan administrator. Of course, when she discovered WON had been incorporated in Delaware, Gwen had also learned that the nefarious Matrix was also WON's registered agent. This time, she would concentrate on researching the WON company.

Gwen finished eating and took her laptop to the dining room table. She did a broad Internet search using the term

WON International. There was a Won International Company, Ltd., based out of South Korea. That made it a near match, but the all-caps of WON felt more like an acronym. Could it be Wood, Onyx, Nickel? We Own Naught? William O, N-something? We Offer Nuts?

Her mind was short-circuiting. It was after 8:00 p.m., Gwen's usual bedtime. Still, there was one more thing to check.

Nothing in the Pension Benefit Guaranty Corporation under the name Won or WON. She even searched the database of orphaned accounts again for Gabe's name. Still nothing.

WON wasn't listed as a Wyoming company, either.

One more shot…

She searched just the word WON. There were numerous hits. One being that *won* was the money currency used in South Korea. That made sense with what she had found, but it still didn't get Gwen anywhere.

Tomorrow she would try the number for Matrix again. Sure, Stuckley would be seeking information through his own channels. But she didn't want to give up on her search. This time, if she didn't get the man who had tried to warn her off, maybe someone else would be willing to talk to her.

Thursday and Friday at the restaurant were a repeat of the previous two days: the early morning rush of hungry farmers and ranchers eager for their day to begin, followed by office workers, sales clerks, business staff, and hungry tourists. It slowed long enough for Gwen and Lacey to clear tables and wrap silverware, and then the early lunch crowd started trickling in the door.

At two on Friday afternoon, Gwen turned it over to the evening shift and went back to her office. There were three voicemail messages. One was a produce supplier following up on an invoice they had sent earlier. The other two were inquiries about the waitress job. Gwen called the women back and set times for the next afternoon to interview them. She told the produce supplier the check had been sent two days earlier.

Like yesterday, she grabbed the daily lunch special and took it home to eat. Belly full, she set back to her digging.

"Hello. I talked to someone a few days ago about a company, WON International," Gwen said when a Matrix operator answered her call. "I didn't get his name. This is about a pension account my late husband had. I understand WON is, or was, the plan's administrator. Is there someone I can talk to?"

"Hold, and I'll transfer you," the voice said.

Gwen listened for nuances that would hint of a warning her call was being forwarded to a person who would likely once again bite her head off, but the voice remained cool and level. There were clicks on the line, a few minutes of music.

Then what sounded like the same man Gwen had talked to earlier, said a gruff, "Hello."

The first time Gwen had been transferred, she had been taken aback when Mr. Grumpy told her the funds had been disbursed and the matter closed. This time, she was better prepared.

"I talked to you a few days ago about my husband's pension with Rhett Manufacturing. His name was Gabe Lindstrom. We lived in Casper—that's in Wyoming—when Gabe worked for Rhett. That was before we moved to Dubois. My husband is deceased, and I'm checking to see what happened to his pension. Do you remember me?"

Silence came through the line, although Gwen could hear breathing. She hurried on.

"From what I understand, any lost pension accounts are supposed to be transferred to the Pension Benefit Guaranty Corporation. I've checked, but neither my late husband's name, nor the company name, is listed."

The last came out in a rush, thwarting any chance for the man to cut her off.

"Like I told you before, that matter was closed years ago." There was an edge of anger in the man's gruff voice.

"And like I said," Gwen growled, echoing his condescension, "Gabe worked hard for that money, and I aim to find out what happened to it."

"Can I get your address?" Mr. Grumpy asked in a more agreeable voice.

Now we're getting somewhere. Gwen spelled out her address and her name.

Just as quickly, the frosty voice resumed. "As I've tried to explain to you earlier, all the fund assets were disbursed. Your husband probably didn't tell you. Who knows why. Not the first time that has happened."

"Wait just a minute," Gwen barked. "No matter what you claim, we never kept secrets from each other. When was that money disbursed? I need to see a copy of the check."

"You're not the account holder," he snapped, "and I don't need to furnish you with anything."

"Really? I've already hired an investigator to look into it, and I bet, between him and my attorney, I'll get answers. What's your name again?"

"Leave it the fuck alone, or else."

"Or else what?" Gwen shouted.

Bang! Like a receiver being slammed into the phone cradle.

What in the hell just happened? Gwen shivered. She got up and started pacing the kitchen.

Something in the man's threat had shot a bolt of ice down her spine. What the hell kind of company was Matrix that they could say something so unprofessional. So intimidating.

Gwen poured a glass of water and gulped it down, suddenly parched. She picked up the cell phone and dialed April.

"That doesn't sound right," April said, after Gwen explained what the man had told her. "And you're sure Gabe never received the proceeds? I know, I know," she said, sensing Gwen was winding up for a retort about Gabe never keeping that information from her. "Did the Matrix employee say when or where the check was sent? Do you think Gabe might have rolled the funds into an IRA account after he left the company, and forgot about it?"

"No," Gwen snarled.

"I believe you," April said, hearing the heat in the one-word answer. "You called the private investigator I recommended?"

"Yes. I haven't heard anything back from him yet."

"Might want to update him on what you were told. Richard's good at what he does, and he has access to a variety of inside contacts and non-public investigative databases. You might also want to talk to the attorney who helped you settle my brother's estate."

"Already on it," Gwen said, before she disconnected.

It was after 6:00 p.m. Gwen would wait and call the attorney tomorrow. The PI might still be working. Did private investigators keep regular hours? Not from what Gwen had seen in movies and on television.

She decided to try. If nothing else, she could leave a voice message.

He picked up on the second ring. "Stuckley Investigations."

"Hi, Richard. It's Gwen Lindstrom. Hey, I have an update for you. Do you have a minute?"

Gwen explained what had happened when she called Matrix.

"So he still didn't give you his name?"

"No."

"And you say you went through the Matrix receptionist to talk to him?"

"Yes, she put me on hold for a brief time, and then he was on the line."

A pause.

"Hmmm. That aligns with some information I discovered," Richard said.

"Meaning?"

"I'm still digging, but I think there's something underhanded going on with that company."

"Meaning?" Gwen repeated.

"Meaning, there is some other stuff I need to check on first. When I talked to you before, did you say you're off work on Mondays?"

"Yes, Monday is my regular day off."

"Feel like a drive to Casper? I could drive to Dubois, but I can't get away from some other things I have going on, until later next week."

"I'll make the drive," Gwen said. "But if it's easier, you can email me. Or I have a fax number for my work, if that's better for you."

"No, no. Better I go over what I found with you in person. It's likely I'll learn more before we meet. You faxed me the last pension statement, but if you have other statements or documents, I can use copies of those, too."

"All right," Gwen said. "Monday it is."

Richard gave her his address—a home office—and they ended their call.

The days were long, this being midsummer. Gwen was too restless for sleep, so she exchanged the sandals she had slipped on, for a pair of tennis shoes and went for a walk.

It took her a while to quiet her thoughts. But soon, she was striding along, breathing fresh air and watching the scenery change to shades of gray and black as the sun set.

The thought of meeting with Stuckley and learning what he had discovered—at least *someone* had discovered *something*—helped bring Gwen some calm.

13

NEAR MISS

By 1:00 p.m., the detectives had mined every grain of information about Gwen's involvement with the private investigator, the reason why she had come to see Stuckley that morning, and what she had seen, done, and touched at his house.

She was starving by the time the detectives finally told her she was free to go. The coffee and donut holes she had eaten earlier were only a vague memory. On the way out of town, she went to the drive-through of a fast-food restaurant, and not wanting to waste anymore of the lost day, drove while she munched on the burger and fries.

Halfway back to Dubois, and feeling re-energized, she gave April a call.

"Ah, shit!" April said, after Gwen updated her about the investigator. "So they're looking at a possible murder, versus an accidental or natural death for Richard?"

"That would be my guess. When I looked through the sliding door to the deck, all I could see was the back of the recliner and his arm—or someone's arm—hanging over the side. I didn't go inside to get a view from the front, and the officers aren't telling me anything, so I'm not sure what happened. There was a pool of something dark on the floor beside the chair, and a smear of what looked like blood on the glass slider. The television was the only light in the room, and my eyes hadn't adjusted, but I'm thinking what was on the floor was blood, too. Are you planning to contact the Casper police to find out what happened? Richard told me he had found something significant when we talked on the phone, but he didn't explain further. I'd like to know what it was. Will they tell you anything?"

"Doubt it, since the local Casper PD has jurisdiction," April said, "and I don't have a pony in the race. But Richard was a friend and a good investigator. Damn it. I'd sure like to know what happened."

"Me, too. I hope it didn't have to do with my case. And I hope they catch the son-of-a-bitch."

Undoubtedly, it had to do with another case the investigator was working on, not Gabe's fifteen-year-old lost pension money, April had told Gwen.

Still, she had woken up the next morning in a somber mood. They were busy at the café, so she didn't even have a chance to stew in her foul temperament. There were customers to take care of, tables to clear, and town gossip to explore.

"Sorry to hear what happened," both Lacey and Mack told her, after Gwen explained what had occurred in Casper.

They did not know Richard or her late husband, and were not invested in the problem. So except for an acknowledgment of what had happened, they had little to say on the matter.

About old wandering cats, however, that was different.

Tuesday flowed into Wednesday as Gwen worried about what had happened to Stuckley. Busy with customers, she and Lacey grazed on breakfast when they had a chance. There was no word from Casper PD on their investigation. Gwen wasn't sure if that was bad or good news. Bad because they hadn't caught the killer. Good because they hadn't come to talk to her. Even April couldn't dig an update out of them.

Carolyn Hubbard arrived about the time the afternoon shift took over. It was *déjà vu*. She looked as frazzled and hot as she had been the first time her cat went missing. Gwen and Lacey shared a look, each knowing what must have happened.

Carolyn said, "I know this seems like a *déjà vu* moment, but Callie is missing again. I can't find her anywhere."

"Miss Callie needs to stay inside," Lacey retorted.

"I know. I tried. But last night, I went out late to retrieve something from my car, and zip. She slipped out right behind me." Carolyn picked up a napkin and dabbed her hairline where droplets of sweat had appeared. "All I saw was the tip of her tail slip away as she rounded the corner of the house."

"We'll come help as soon as the afternoon staff arrives," Gwen heard herself say.

"Did you look in the lot where we found her last time?" Lacey said.

"I already did. And thank you both for finding her before. I just hate to be such a burden."

"You're not a burden." Lacey patted Carolyn on the shoulder.

An hour later, Lacey and Gwen had finished work and were walking toward the vacant lot behind Carolyn's house.

Carolyn came out of her home when she saw them arrive, looking as anxious as she had been earlier.

"I'll check over by the trees." Lacey headed toward the back of the lot.

"Gwen, if you don't mind, can you check around that old house foundation? I don't see so well anymore, and I'm always afraid of tripping over stuff."

"Sure." Gwen started toward where she had searched last time.

The afternoon was hot. Gwen had put on a cap to protect her face from the sun, but soon the heat seeped through the cloth hat, and her shirt was sticking to her back.

She scanned left and right as she walked, occasionally adding her calls for Callie to the ones Carolyn and Lacey made.

"Hey, Callie girl," she crooned, as she picked her way through the crumbled stone cabin.

A breeze picked up, rustling leaves high in the trees, and providing a welcomed relief to the oven of the day.

Gwen glimpsed a lift of white and black fur and started toward it.

"You little sneak," she said, when she found the cat.

Callie was curled against a shaded corner of the broken foundation like she had fallen asleep. But when Gwen came closer, she saw a fly move across one of the cat's half-closed eyelids, and realized the cat must have died.

Poor old thing curled up for a slumber, and the slumber became permanent. Not a bad way to go, if one thought about it.

Gwen bent to smooth the long fur. Before her fingers could touch the cat, she heard the crack of a gunshot. Something slammed into the wall above her head, and rock chips rained down.

"Get down!" Lacey shouted.

Gwen dropped to her knees and scrambled around the sole standing corner of the abandoned house as another shot sounded, and another shatter of stone dust rained down.

Rifle shots, one part of her mind registered. Time seemed to halt, although it must have just been a brief moment. In the silence, Gwen heard the sound of her panicked breathing.

A third shot cracked, and from a different direction, a shotgun boomed.

Gwen took a shaky breath, and two more. Her heart raced, and heat flashed through her chest.

After what seemed like forever, she heard a car door slam, a motor gun, and tires screech away.

What the hell just happened? Discordant thoughts pinged

around Gwen's brain. Was the owner of the abandoned lot mad at their trespass? Did the three of them look like deer or a flock of ducks? Did someone poison Callie, and feared the deed would be discovered?

"They're gone!" a deep voice shouted. "You okay, Miss Carolyn?"

"I'm good, Clyde," she answered in a shaky voice.

Gwen heard a shuffle of feet and turned to see Lacey stumbling toward her. Gwen was still crouched down, afraid to stand. Afraid her trembling legs wouldn't hold her up.

"You okay, Gwen?" Lacey said, her voice pitched higher than usual.

"I'm good. But what—"

"Fuck if I know," Lacey said.

Then she spied Callie, still curled in eternal slumber.

"Oh, poor thing. Did she get hit? I'm going to kill—"

"No, no." Gwen held up her hand in a stop gesture. "Callie was gone before the shooting began. I started to pick her up. Then…" She shivered, felt dizzy.

When she looked at where she had been standing, Gwen saw a fresh pockmark on the corner wall where her head had been. At that, her legs did give out, and her vision went dark.

"Oh my!" she heard Carolyn say from far away.

———

Gwen returned to her body to find Carolyn holding a glass of ice water for her to drink. Lacey was there with a concerned look on her face as she wrung out a washcloth and placed it on Gwen's forehead. Clyde, neighbor and operator of the shotgun that had scared the shooter off, was heading out of the lot, a towel-wrapped object in his arms.

"Sorry about your cat," Gwen croaked, embarrassed about blacking out.

Carolyn waved in a dismissive fashion. Tears welled up in the corners of her eyes, and she didn't speak for a moment.

"I'll miss the old girl. But Lacey said it looked like she just curled up and went to sleep. That cat always loved exploring. Here. I brought you some ice water. Lacey's already called the law. They should be here—"

A wail of sirens announced two arriving vehicles. First, the four-wheel-drive SUV that April drove for work. And the second, a vehicle with a badge decal on the door, identifying it as the Dubois City Police.

April strode toward them, face in a grimace and splotched red.

"God damn it, are you okay?" she asked Gwen, the center of the knot of people who had gathered around.

"I'm okay, really." Gwen got up to stand on shaky legs, and dusted off the seat of her pants.

April, normally in control, and always mindful of her position as sheriff, hauled Gwen close and gave her a tight squeeze.

"I'm good, really," Gwen said. "It's just that…I'm having trouble breathing." She said this to both reassure her sister-in-law she really was fine, and to relieve the tension of April's death-grip hug.

The sheriff released her, but examined Gwen, cap to canvas shoes.

"Well, that's a relief," April said. "I wouldn't want my brother to haunt me to the end of my days because I didn't take care of his wife."

She took a step back, and was once again in sheriff mode.

"Anyone get a view of the shooter?" she snapped.

Carolyn and Lacey shook their heads.

Clyde replied, "Black SUV. Looked like a late-model Lincoln or Suburban, but I wasn't close enough to be sure. The driver stayed inside. Didn't get a good look at him. The passenger was the shooter. He was average height and weight. Had a cap pulled low so I couldn't see his face clearly. Dark hair below the back of the cap. Didn't catch the license plate of the vehicle. Rifle, but I couldn't discern the make. That's all I know."

The Dubois officer recorded all the information in a notebook.

"Clyde used to be a game warden up near Yellowstone," Carolyn said.

April nodded. "This helps."

She stepped away and spoke into her phone.

More officers arrived, and they set out examining the scene. Lacey and Gwen were relegated to deck chairs on Carolyn's back porch, where they watched the activity. Clyde joined them with a pitcher of icy lemonade and plastic cups.

"Anyone know where the third shot landed?" Gwen went over the event in her mind. "The first two hit the standing corner of the old stone house."

If I hadn't bent over to look at the cat...

She shivered.

Carolyn shook her head.

Lacey said, "I was behind a tree, so I didn't see."

"That was about the time I stepped out the back door with the shotgun," Clyde said. "Could be, the shooter saw me and the last shot went wild."

But the first two shots had been aimed at Gwen, and that made her check the door locks twice that night at home and pull the curtains tight. It kept her awake in the dark for a long time.

Did Richard's murderer think she saw something that identified him as the shooter? Did it have to do with the Ranchers Café? Or did this have something to do with her poking into what had happened to Gabe's money?

Exhaustion finally pulled her into a restless sleep haunted by dreams of being chased by a faceless shooter.

14

VICKERS AND MYERS

Gwen would have given anything to be able to call in sick the next day. Her head ached, and her body was sore like she really had spent the night fleeing an attacker. The bathroom mirror revealed that she looked the same as she felt. But she was co-owner of the cafe, and at 4:30 in the morning, there was no one she could call to take her shift.

"This is why it doesn't pay to be the boss," she grumbled, as she poured a cup of coffee and went to get ready.

"Boss, you're taking the customers in the back of the restaurant today," Lacey announced when she arrived.

Gwen shook her head as she washed down aspirins with more coffee. She didn't want to endanger Lacey. The restaurant had a front wall of glass windows with a view of the parking lot. That meant she and the other wait staff were visible from a long distance. Worse, Gwen worried about the customers. If she did work the back tables, and the shooter was determined, how many people would be in the line of a bullet aimed at her?

At least the kitchen staff would be safe. They were tucked behind a wall and not visible from the parking lot.

"No," Gwen replied. "Let's just do our normal routine. I'll

pull down the sunshades. My biggest worry is the customers. Honestly, I thought hard about closing today."

"We can still do that," Lacey said.

But by then, customers eager for breakfast were arriving.

One of the first visitors was Sheriff April Erickson. Following in her wake were two men in khaki pants and blue short-sleeved shirts. Both had guns holstered at their hips.

"Investigators Vickers and Myers from the Wyoming Division of Criminal Investigation," April told Gwen. "They would like to talk to you."

"I got 'em," Lacey told Gwen, in regard to the three tables of customers in the restaurant.

Gwen led April and the two investigators down the hall to her office. The space was small, and four people made it a tight squeeze.

"Tell us what you know," Vickers told Gwen.

"I don't know what it's all about, really. Don't know if this is because of Richard Stuckley's other cases, and his killer thought I saw something that would implicate him. Or if it has something to do with me."

"Let's start with why you contacted the PI," Vickers said.

Gwen explained how she had found Gabe's old pension statements, and what she discovered on her own about the company that bought out Rhett Manufacturing. She told them about contacting Matrix, and what the rude man had told her, including the threat.

At the mention of Matrix, she noticed Myers—who had relaxed back into one of the chairs they had brought in—straightened and listened more intently. She also noticed their expressions didn't change when she told them about finding Richard. They must have already talked to the Casper detectives. No doubt the two investigators knew more about that than she did.

"We were looking for Carolyn Hubbard's cat when someone

shot at me," Gwen said. "I realized last night that the Matrix guy had asked for my home address. I thought it was because he was sending me a claim form. Do you think this is all connected?"

The two investigators shared a look.

Then Vickers replied, "The Matrix connection interests us. The firm has been on our radar for a while. That's all I can tell you now." He turned to April. "What I can say is that you all need to take precautions." He turned his attention back to Gwen. "This working out in the open," he waved toward the front of the cafe, "is not a good thing. Sheriff," he returned his focus to April, "we'll be around for a couple days. But that's not going to help Ms. Lindstrom here."

"You need to get someone to cover your shift," April told Gwen. "At least until this is resolved. And you need to keep out of sight."

"Well, hell!" Gwen said. "And what am I supposed to do?"

"First, I need to see the pension statements and any information you developed," Vickers said. "We can meet you at your house, go over it. You mentioned you talked to the executive assistant of the company who took over Rhett."

"Yes. Katherine Saunders. She started with Rhett, and then continued with the new company. At least, for a while. I called her, but she told me she had signed some kind of confidentiality agreement, so couldn't talk to me."

"She'll talk to us." Myers said as he jotted her name in the notebook he had been using to document their conversation.

"We'll need her number," Vickers said. "You have that here?"

"At home," Gwen said. "Let me call a couple people. See if they can come in and take my place for a few days." She paused for a moment. "There's the staff and our customers. I'm more concerned about them. You think I should just close the restaurant for a few days?"

"You do what you feel is best," Vickers said, which was the most unhelpful advice Gwen had heard for a long while.

April said, "You're the target. Nothing else indicates otherwise. Lacey and Carolyn were with you in the lot yesterday, but the shots were aimed at you."

"Well, two were," Gwen said, recalling her terror that day.

"We found the third in a tree," April said, "and we're analyzing the bullet now. The other two shattered when they hit stone. I suspect Clyde threw the shooter off his game. Otherwise, the third would have also been aimed your way."

"Too bad Clyde wasn't a better shot," Gwen grumbled.

"Yeah, but a shotgun doesn't have the range of a rifle," April told her. "What I'm getting at is, with you out of the picture—and you know, word travels fast around here—Lacey and the customers should be safe. I recommend, at least for the rest of today, that you close. They're not after the restaurant. They are after you. My deputies and I will do a drive-by every hour or so for the next few days to ferret out any suspicious people or vehicles."

"Ready to go?" Vickers asked Gwen.

"Give me a minute to phone around and get someone to cover me for a few days. I promise I'll stay back here in the office."

"Works for me," Myers said. "In fact, that bacon smelled real good when we came in."

"You're right about that," Vickers agreed. "We'll order something to eat. It'll give us a chance to observe the lot while you make the calls. We're parked right outside. Our car's not marked, but it has multiple antennae, and that identifies it as a law enforcement vehicle. It should keep the threat away. If they're still around. When you're ready, we'll follow you to your house."

15

GETAWAY PLAN

The parade of Gwen in her Jeep, and the two investigators in a black Suburban, wound through the streets to Gwen's home. Before she left, Gwen told them she planned to take a circuitous route, just in case someone was following. They had nodded their approval.

When Gwen pulled into her drive, there was a note attached to her door. She got out of the car and moved toward it. Vickers and Myers jumped out of their car and rushed past her.

"Stay here for a minute while we take a look." Myers spread an arm back toward her in a wait gesture.

After an inspection of the piece of paper, they ushered Gwen inside. She tried not to roll her eyes, but she had already seen the familiar red and blue logo indicating it was from the post office.

Myers went to pick up the package USPS was holding for Gwen. Vickers stayed behind.

"You want some coffee?" she said.

"Sure."

Gwen went to brew it while trying to think what the package could be. She hadn't ordered anything lately.

Soon, Myers was back, packet in hand.

Stuckley, the return address said, and listed a Casper box number. Now she was well and truly puzzled.

Again, she had to wait until the investigators examined the package and cut the envelope open. Inside was a letter, a packet of documents, and a flash drive. She bent to pick up the letter, but Myers put a hand on her arm to stop her. Vickers was already putting on the latex gloves he had pulled from his pocket.

"Don't want to contaminate these if there are fingerprints." He laid the letter on the edge of the table so she could read it.

Gwen,

Discovered information that concerns me. In the process, I suspect I triggered a spy trap. Had some calls and other things happen that make me concerned for my safety and yours. For that reason, enclosed is what I have gathered, along with a recording of my conversation with Katherine Saunders, former secretary for Rhett. This may be all for naught, but I will explain more when I see you on Monday.

It was dated the Saturday before she went to see him.

Her eyes stung, and she went to get a tissue to wipe them. It was such a strange and sad experience. Here, Richard was telling her he was looking forward to explaining what he had discovered. And between mailing the package and Monday, someone had murdered him, with their business unfinished. Worse, she felt guilty for getting him involved. Was finding Gabe's money worth it? It didn't seem fair—not to Stuckley's family, and not to her.

Vickers and Myers, who had been reading over her shoulder, shared a look Gwen couldn't decipher.

"You have a copy machine here?" Vickers asked.

"Sure. It's in a spare bedroom I use as a home office. Why?"

Vickers turned to Myers. "Go ahead and make copies of what was in the envelope. We'll bag the originals."

"Make a copy for me, too," Gwen said.

Vickers shook his head. "I'm not sure—"

Gwen interrupted. "Listen, that package was addressed to me. I'm the one who hired the PI, and I'm the one who found his body. It's Gabe's account, so you can't just shut me out."

Another look was exchanged between the two men. She hated that silent communication.

"Go ahead," Vickers told Myers, then focused cop eyes on Gwen. "I want you somewhere out of danger. Is there anyone you can stay with for a few days?"

Gwen gave that some thought. She didn't want to endanger her business partner, Mack, or his family. Lacey lived in a one-bedroom apartment over Mack's garage. Not nearly enough room for two women used to the solitude of their own homes.

April—that was out of the question. Sure, April was the sheriff, and no doubt she could defend home and family. But there was no way Gwen wanted to endanger them. Plus, April and her husband had three rowdy boys. Gwen enjoyed visiting, but she also enjoyed coming home and quietly reading.

There was Jay, the funeral director who was her friend and sometimes lover. He might be willing to let her stay with him, but the romantic part of their relationship was new, and she didn't want to hinder its fragile state. More importantly, Jay was still married. Never mind that Lauren had Alzheimer's and lived in a nursing home. Her daughter, Jackie, lived in Colorado, but Gwen was afraid that whoever was after her would quickly figure out that she might take refuge there.

No, there was no one she wanted to put in danger.

"I can't think of anyone," she confessed. "Plus, Dubois is a small town, and I've been active in the community, so it's not like I can just put on a wig and sunglasses and not be recognized."

Myers had came back with the copies. "I understand."

Vickers said, "I know a retired highway patrol captain. Has a cabin maybe thirty minutes outside Dubois. He and his wife are spending the summer in Denver, with their daughter and new baby. Let me call him. See if the agency can rent his cabin." He turned to Gwen. "You pack, Ms. Lindstrom, while I make the call."

Gwen thought she was processing the events of the last few days well, but she found herself in the middle of her bedroom, half-filled suitcase on the bed, forgetting what she needed to do. She hadn't cried since that dreary winter after Gabe died, and by God, she wasn't going to start now. This, she thought while wiping her eyes and blowing her nose with bathroom tissue.

"We're set," Vickers said, when Gwen rolled her suitcase out of the bedroom. We already moved your car into the garage. Let's pull the drapes, and then we'll be ready to go. Oh, almost forgot. The cabin is isolated, but the captain has plenty of books. There is Internet service, and it's a short walk to a good fishing creek."

At that, Gwen added her fishing gear, laptop, two books she wanted to tackle, and they set off.

16

REFUGE IN THE WOODS

Thirty-five miles north of Dubois, on Highway 26, the investigators—with Gwen in the back seat, behind heavily tinted windows—turned onto a blacktopped road. Houses with tin roofs of red, green, and blue dotted the landscape. Both men had been checking the mirrors as Myers drove, to make sure they weren't followed. When they turned onto the road, Vickers swiveled in his seat to observe the nearly empty highway behind them until the trees swallowed them up.

A few miles in, they turned onto a gravel road. The grade changed, winding up and then down through the hills.

"Turn here," Vickers instructed

They pulled into a drive and wound alternatively through strands of pines and meadows of sagebrush.

"You're not kidding this is isolated!" Gwen said.

She had grown up in Wyoming, spent her childhood, and as much of her adult life as possible, in the outdoors. But this time, the isolation felt different. Had the last few weeks tainted her perspective? Or was it because her companions were strangers and she didn't know them well enough to be comfortable? Likely, she just needed quiet and sleep.

A log cabin with a green metal roof came into view. It had been here for a while, not like some of the newer, larger homes she had seen on the journey. The logs had mellowed to a toasty brown, and the roof had a few rusty spots along the eves where the paint had chipped off. Still, the large clearing was neat—split wood stacked under a carport beside a covered outside grill. To one side, an outside prep area waited, ready for the next batch of fish.

Inside, the three-bedroom, one-bath home was just as tidy. There was a large main room with a kitchen to one side, open to the room. Off the main room were three doorways that Gwen could see were two bedrooms separated by a bathroom. Over the kitchen was a loft tall enough for her to stand in, which served as a third bedroom. The loft was open to the main space, and Gwen could see the foot of a bed. No dishes remained in the dish drainer, and books were stacked neatly on a coffee table by a chair.

The cabin had that expected North Woods theme, with moose and bighorn sheep photographs hanging on the walls, and bronze lamps etched with trees and more wildlife. A fireplace fronted with large river rocks was set with logs and ready for a match.

All in all, it was a place Gwen could call home. At least temporarily.

"One of those is the guest room." Vickers motioned toward the downstairs bedrooms. "We'll help carry your stuff and supplies in. Then we need to start back. I want to be back on the highway before dark."

After the two men drove away, quiet settled in the clearing. Gwen unpacked, made an exploratory trip to look at the stream, and heated the dinner she had picked up on the way.

―――

Her first two days at the cabin, Gwen slept and explored the area. There was a low wooden deck out the kitchen door, where she had a morning coffee and perused the news on her laptop. The place did have surprisingly good Internet service, considering it was surrounded by pines, its back to a hill.

The third day, she took her fly fishing pole and gear and hiked down the trail to the creek. It was August and the trees were still green, although the leaves had a frazzled look that hinted of fall.

On the creek, mosquitoes buzzed and Gwen was glad she had applied repellent. The cool stream, low this time of year, burbled, and it didn't take Gwen long to snag a trout from one of the deeper pools. By the time the afternoon had started to fade into evening, she had two plump fish waiting on the line.

After Vickers and Myers told her about the nearby stream, she had packed flour and cornmeal. She cleaned the fish, dipped the filets into a mix of flour and cornmeal, and fried them in a pan with potatoes. After dinner, Gwen read for a while, and then, yawning, put down the book, turned off the lights, and went to ready herself for sleep.

Of course, as soon as the light was turned off and she had settled into a nest of pillows and blankets, worries started pinging around in her head. She worried how the restaurant was fairing with her not there. Mack had told her he'd take care of paying the bills, but had he?

Gwen punched the pillow and flipped the blanket off, suddenly hot.

Had Vickers and Myers learned anything about Stuckley's murder? Would they even tell her what they found? Did Richard Stuckley have children? Brothers or sisters? She should have sent the family condolences, but here she was, stuck without a vehicle, so she couldn't even buy a card.

Giving up, she turned the light back on and read until she found herself dozing mid-paragraph.

17

———————

OR NOT

SOMETIME LATER, GWEN WOKE, SWEATING AND GASPING FOR AIR. In the nightmare, she had been running to escape Vickers and Myers, who were aiming to mow her down with the same black SUV they had used to drive her to the cabin. She lay on her back, taking deep gulps of breath and feeling her heart hammer.

The lighted face of the bedside clock glowed 3:15 a.m. Knowing she wouldn't be able to sleep for a while, Gwen plumped the pillows against the headboard and analyzed the dream.

She, Lacey, and Carolyn were looking for Callie Cat again. Only, this time they were in the woods by the cabin. Somehow they had gotten lost, the trail morphing into a maze of dead ends and false trails. Gwen saw lights in the distance and started toward them, feeling comforted that they had found a way out. Only, it wasn't an escape. A large dark vehicle with blinding headlights hurtled toward them. Myers sat behind the wheel, and Vickers pointed a rifle out the window at her.

There had been a scuffing noise in the dream—something out of place in the hazy terror of escaping a roaring vehicle. In the dream, she had turned toward the noise right before she awoke. Had the scrape and scuff been part of the dream, or a real sound that pulled her back to the dark bedroom?

She listened. There it was. Shuffling footfalls, soft like someone was sneaking across the porch. And just where the hell was her rifle? In the living room, propped in the corner with her fishing rods and tackle.

Should she pull the covers over her head, or go look? The first was not an option, really. Gwen had never been one to shy away from conflict, or to curl up and let the monster under the bed seize her foot.

If it was a gunman coming back to finish the job, she wanted her phone to call 911, and a rifle to hold him off until someone could arrive.

She pushed off the covers but couldn't convince her legs to move. She was as stuck to the bed as the fish had been to the stringer. The slender hope of reaching the phone and rifle before the intruder broke down the door is what finally spurred her to move.

Gwen crept through the dark bedroom, into the living area. There was no assistance from the light of a moon. It had been a thin sliver when she stepped outside earlier to take the trash to the fire pit for burning in the morning.

Scrape, shuffle went something big outside.

With shaking hands, Gwen located the rifle, opened the bolt and felt the chamber to make sure it had a cartridge loaded, and then shut the bolt.

There was a growl outside, and Gwen ducked down, staying in the shadows of the kitchen. If someone was coming after her, would that someone be growling? Either the guy was clumsy, or didn't care that he could be heard.

Another growl.

A memory came to mind. "Shit," she hissed.

Gwen went to the front door and flicked on the porch light.

A half-grown bear, startled by the sudden light, bounded off the porch and toward its mother, who was scavenging the fire pit.

Stupid of her, really, to do something as amateurish as dumping the trout guts and trash in the fire pit, and deciding to wait until morning to burn it all.

Gwen hooked the safety back on the rifle and took it with her to bed. In the now quiet darkness, she went back to examining the dream. What had triggered the connection between the shooter and the two agents? Clyde, Carolyn's neighbor, said the gunman who fired at them was driving a dark SUV. The two agents who had come to talk to her, and then driven her to this isolated cabin, drove a black Chevy Suburban. Just how well had she inspected their ID cards? Not at all. She just took their word that they had been sent by the Wyoming Division of Criminal Investigation. April had brought them to the restaurant and introduced the investigators. Had she checked their identification? Or had both she and April simply assumed—by way of holstered pistols and moxie—that they were legit?

What a perfect setup this was. Cunning killers drive an unsuspecting victim to an isolated place in the woods, and then sneak back to kill her after they set up their alibi. Gwen was like the naive fish in a clear stream, never suspecting the delicious-looking bait held a barbed hook.

She looked at the time—3:45 a.m. April might be able to verify the agents' credentials, but Gwen couldn't call her at this hour without giving her sister-in-law a heart attack. She could do something else, though.

She molded pillows on the bed in the spare room—the one the agents had led her to—into what she hoped passed for her body, and arranged the covers over it. Still leaving the lights off, she made sure the doors were locked and double bolted, and the windows locked as well. Then she took her rifle and the box of extra ammunition and climbed the stairs to the open loft. If someone did manage to break in, both her location, and that she was armed, would be a surprise and a deterrent.

Gwen propped the pillows in the loft bed against the far wall and leaned against them, intending to keep watch the rest of the night. There was no clock up here, and she didn't want to alert a watcher by checking the time on her lighted phone screen, so after what seemed like forever, she pulled up the covers against the chill. *Just for a minute.* She closed her eyes.

The next thing she knew, dawn was seeping in, and sunlight in her eyes woke her.

The first thing she did was peer over the loft railing. Everything looked the same as it had the evening before.

She made the bed and then took the rifle downstairs, where she used the restroom and started the coffeemaker. Then she called April.

"Sure, I met the two investigators," the sheriff said, as Gwen took her coffee outside to the back deck. "They came by our office to check in before we came to talk to you. Why?"

"Nothing that seems logical by the light of day," Gwen said. "Had a nightmare last night, and you know how one's mind can make strange connections when dreaming. The gunman who shot at me, and the Wyoming DCI agents, both drive the same kind of vehicle—big, black, and intimidating."

April laughed. "I can see why you made the connection. Both sides of the law seem to favor that type of vehicle. I didn't doubt who they said they were, but let me call the DCI office and confirm. I'll get back to you. That should save you any night-time creepy thoughts."

"Thanks." Gwen sighed, relief flooding through her.

Really, it was just a nightmare, and the connection seemed idiotic in the daylight. Still…

Ten minutes later, April called back.

"You can rest easy. Both the badge numbers and descriptions fit the men."

"That's a relief," Gwen said.

"One thing." April's tone became serious. "You've been using your cell phone, right?"

"Yes."

"And you used that number when you were calling Matrix to find out what happened with Gabe's money?"

"Sure."

"We have the ability to track the location of a cell phone if we have the number. My guess—the bad guys can do the same. And faster since they don't require a warrant to track someone down. Keep your phone off. You can turn it back on for a few minutes this evening—let's say six o'clock—and call me so I know you're all right. I'll also update you on any progress. It'll only take a few minutes."

"But then they can track me."

"It's possible in those few minutes, but let's make you a less visible target by keeping the phone off. I'll call Vickers and see if he can run a throw-away phone to you."

Gwen turned off the phone and put it on the charger. She was getting tired of this game. Of not knowing what was really going on. And of having to hide away like a trapped rat.

Time to take charge.

SCHEME EXPOSED

Gwen refilled her coffee cup, grabbed the copies of what she had received in the mail from Richard, and spread them out on the kitchen breakfast bar. She would have liked a copy of what had been on the flash drive, but Vickers and Myers had taken it, along with the original documents.

Some of the information she had already discovered: the sale of Rhett Manufacturing to McMasters–Bryant, and then later to RHM Enterprises. Richard had also discovered that the owners of RHM Enterprises, Inc., EC Holdings, LP, and Maritime, Inc., and the plan administrator, WON International, all had Matrix in common. He had printed out the incorporation documents of all the entities, as well as created a chart showing the connections between companies and principals.

The new information to her was a list of all pension plan account holders Rhett had at the time the company was sold. Sixty-three accounts, Gwen counted. After some of them, Richard had written in addresses and phone numbers. Before the names, he had penciled in D, UK, and checkmarks. The D meant deceased, Gwen figured out when she saw the letter before Gabe's name. She guessed the UK meant unknown. Did that mean Richard couldn't locate the person? Or did it mean something else?

The names with checkmarks before them had two dollar amounts at the end of the name—a higher amount and a lesser amount. There were ten more names with stars beside them. Gwen couldn't figure the meaning of the marks and dollar amounts until she took a closer look and found Mark Tankerson's name with a checkmark beside it and two figures—$84,680 and $49,475.

Earlier, when she had talked to Lynn Tankerson, Gwen learned that WON had taken close to half of Mark's pension for various taxes and fees. She needed a calculator to be sure, but it looked like the difference between the two figures was close to one-half.

Gwen searched the two drawers of the desk that sat in a corner of the living area. No calculator there. She searched through a drawer in the kitchen that held miscellaneous items. Nothing.

If she didn't make a phone call, would turning on her cell phone and using the calculator app trigger GPS tracking?

Gwen returned to the accounts list and reviewed all the check-marked items. She decided that if the bad guys didn't have her location by now, they probably couldn't determine it in the few minutes it would take her to use the phone's calculator. So she took the phone off the charging cord, turned it on, and took it back to where she had been working.

Four minutes later—she timed it—the phone was back off and she had her answer. That is, if what Lynn had said about the deductions was the explanation for the differing amounts.

WON had carved out a sum of $188,497, just from what Richard had discovered. Hell of a lot of fees, taxes, and so-called research costs. Moreover, had the amount taken out for taxes even been turned over to the IRS? She didn't have access to that kind of information. Could Myers and Vickers ask the IRS?

And what about the accounts marked with a D? Were they like Gabe—the surviving family didn't realize, or had forgotten, that their loved ones were owed money? Would the survivors have made a claim, or like Gwen, been caught in the morass of companies and given up.

The company, the owners, the account administrator all led back to Matrix, and that's where she had encountered the gruff-voiced threat.

So the WON deductions Richard had found amounted to six figures. Taking into account the deceased pensioners and the accounts not located, WON could have easily walked away with close to a million dollars. That might be enough justification to kill Richard and shoot at her.

The knowledge made her stomach roil, and the once welcoming cabin now felt like a trap. She had been here long enough with her phone—and GPS—operational that someone would have been able to locate her. Gwen needed to call the investigators and April with what she had learned. She needed to get the hell out of here. Next time, it might not be a bear that came hunting in the night.

She turned the cell phone back on and dialed the number Vickers had given her. It rang and rang and then went to voicemail. She ended the call before leaving a message. The nightmare still tainted her confidence in the two men, even though April had confirmed their employment.

She tried April's cell. It, too, went to voicemail.

Now Gwen was really worried. It wasn't like April to ignore her phone. What if something terrible had happened, and here she was, goofing off in the woods.

It was past noon, and Gwen went outside and listened for sounds that didn't belong. She heard nothing but birds chatting in the trees, and the soft sound of a breeze through pine branches.

Why couldn't this retired captain have built his home on a

hill so she could survey the area? No, the man built his cozy little cabin in a valley surrounded by woods so he could be close to fishing spots. *Damn.*

Gwen went back inside, cleaned the kitchen, and put away the washed dishes. Then she went and tidied the bathroom, stripped the bed, and started a washer of towels and sheets. By the time the bedding was in the dryer, it was after two o'clock.

She turned the phone back on and went through the list again: Vickers, Myers, and April. Still, no one answered. Still, she did not leave voicemails.

Gwen rummaged around in the desk again, this time finding what she was looking for. On a bill for the owner was the cabin's address. *Making progress.* She turned on the phone once again and pulled up Lacey's number from the contact list.

"Gwen?" Lacey answered in a hesitant voice.

"Yes. Hi, Lacey." Gwen tried to keep her voice calm. "Just checking in to see how things are going at the restaurant."

"A little hectic, but we're doing okay. How about you?"

"Bored. Very bored. All I've done is sleep."

A shadowing of the truth. But describing the nightmare and what she had discovered about the theft seemed excessive for a casual conversation.

Lacey chuckled. "Sleep doesn't sound half-bad. How much longer do they want you to stay away?"

"Actually, I'm ready to come back, but I can't seem to reach the two investigators. The ones that came to the restaurant. Have you seen them lately?"

"Nooo." Lacey answered, drawing out the word. "Last time I saw them was two days ago. They said they had to go back to Cheyenne, but didn't say why."

"Hmm. How about Sheriff Erickson? Seen her lately?"

"No. Come to think of it, she comes in once in a while, but it's usually to talk to you. Why do you ask?

"Nothing. Just wondering how things were going."

Lacey took a deep breath. "Well, Mack said he's gotten some calls lately, and asked me if I'd received any weird ones."

"Weird like what?" Gwen's felt chilled all of a sudden.

"He didn't say much. Just people trying to reach you. But I think he's worried about something."

Gwen wanted—needed—to get back. She'd show everyone what she had discovered, and the need for secrecy would be moot.

"You mind doing me a favor?" Gwen said, after a minute.

"Sure. Name it."

"I need someone to pick me up. I'll pay for gas and your time. You have a GPS on your phone?"

"Hey, no problem. And don't worry about gas. I owe you big time, anyway, after you helped me after Donny died."

Donny was the boyfriend who had been murdered earlier by poachers and drug couriers who had used their barn to store contraband.

Gwen gave Lacey the cabin address and directions to where they had turned off the highway. Lacey promised she'd be there as soon as she could after she got off work.

Gwen went to pack her belongings.

19

DANGEROUS COMPANY

Two hours later, Lacey arrived to find Gwen waiting on the porch, luggage and gear beside her.

Lacey got out of the car and opened the trunk. "Are you sure it's okay to come back home?"

"If I could reach the DCI guys and tell them what I found, I'm sure they could get an arrest. Then I don't have to hide. Problem is, they're not answering their damn phones," Gwen said, through gritted teeth.

She had done their work—figured out what WON, or Matrix, or whoever, was doing—but here she was, stuck in an isolated cabin, waiting for a gunman to come after her.

Lacey, reading Gwen's frustration, quickly lifted the bags into the trunk.

"Anything we need to do inside?" she said.

"Nope."

Lacey gave her boss a searching look, and then they both climbed in and fastened their seat belts. Between her feet, Gwen tucked a small duffel that contained, among the shampoo and soaps, a pistol.

Twice on the way back to Dubois, Gwen tried calling the

investigators and April, but cell phone reception was sketchy in this part of the country, and the calls didn't ring through. Finally, she gave up.

"Well, tell me what's been going on at the restaurant?"

Lacey filled her in, told her the new wait staff was working out. "But slow," she added. "Everyone is asking about you. I told them what you said, that you took a brief vacation, but that just invited more questions. Anyway, so you're back for good now?"

"Not quite. I still need to talk with the two DCI agents, but I'm back home. Just don't let anyone know it yet."

Gwen thought for a minute.

"Have there been any new customers, different from our normal ones?"

"Like?"

"Like, maybe they're not dressed like tourists. Or they look like one of those mob gangsters."

"No mobsters. Hard to say about the rest. It's tourist season, so there are lots of people I don't know." Lacey grinned. "Only one strange was a guy that came in with a moose hat. You know the kind. Fake fur, with little antlers sticking out each side."

"Oh, that's funny," Gwen said.

It felt good to laugh. The thought of moose hat man meeting a real moose, one with an attitude about the hat, left her in a good mood all the way to her house.

April buzzed her on the phone as Lacey turned onto Gwen's street.

"I saw you called."

"I've been trying to reach you all day," Gwen said. "Something happen?"

"Continuing ed and firearm certification," the sheriff grumbled. "Cell phones had to be off. What's up with you?"

"Couple things. I think I figured out what's going on and why whoever it is doesn't want anyone to know."

Gwen explained Richard's notes beside the list of pensioners, and what she thought it meant.

"So you're saying someone is running a scheme to steal money out of the retirement accounts?"

"That's what it looks like. Richard didn't get a chance to contact everyone on the list. I ran a calculation of what he found. They—WON or Matrix—collected six figures worth of fees, taxes, and research costs. I'm also betting the taxes they collected on early withdrawals never made it to the IRS."

"You told Vickers and Myers this?" April asked.

"I haven't been able to reach them. Do you know where they are?"

"Last time I talked to Vickers, he said they were headed to Cheyenne to try to convince Katherine Saunders to talk to them."

There was a pause in the conversation while each thought over what had been said.

Then the sheriff said, "You said two things. What was the other one?"

"I'm back home. In fact, I'm sitting in Lacey's car, in my driveway."

"What!" April shouted. "Why in the hell—"

"Because I was bored out there. And because that's the worst place to be if someone is after me. Hell, the cabin is in a valley. Between that and the trees, I wouldn't be able to see if someone was coming."

"Dang it, Gwen. Go to a motel or go stay with Jay until I get back into town. Jesus Christ, you're just sitting in the car, out in the open?"

"Calm down. I doubt they're after me. I'm just a little mouse nibbling at a part of what they're doing."

"They likely killed Richard." April pronounced each word slowly, like Gwen was a difficult child.

"I'll be fine, really. I'll just drop my stuff off and give Jay a call."

Gwen didn't believe she was in any real danger. No doubt, they had already been by her house and work and discovered she was gone. Still, she surveyed the street before she got out and keyed in the code that opened the garage door.

Lacey helped her carry her bags inside the garage, then said goodbye and left, and Gwen was gloriously back in her own home.

She checked to see if anything was out of place. The garage was the same. Her Jeep was still where the agents had parked it. Nothing appeared out of place when she carried her suitcase and equipment inside the house.

First, she stowed the fishing gear in the room off the garag, took the suitcase and rifle case to her bedroom, and then remembered she needed to call Vickers and let him know she was back home. She rang his number, and this time when no one answered, she left a message saying she was back home and asked him to call her.

Were they still in Cheyenne? Katherine must have blabbed if it was taking this long.

Gwen realized after she unpacked and threw dirty clothing in the hamper that she was starving. She searched the freezer but found no frozen dinners. The milk in her fridge smelled sour, so she poured it down the drain. The two remaining eggs were questionable. She ended up pouring cereal into a bowl and adding condensed milk she mixed with water.

Gwen was rinsing out the bowl when she heard a vehicle. She walked to the front door, wiping her hands on a towel. The window curtains were still closed, and mindful of April's admonishment to be careful, she peeked out one of the wavy glass panels in the front door. A large black vehicle had pulled into the drive.

"Vickers and Myers," she muttered. "Great that they called to let me know they were coming."

Unless, of course, they had picked up her message and were pissed she was back home. Tough luck. They should have answered their phones.

She was about to open the door and tell them just that, when she realized the two men exiting the vehicle didn't look like Vickers and Myers. The wavy glass distorted her view, but to her, the passenger was too tall and bulky to be Vickers. He started toward the garage, which Gwen instantly realized she had failed to close after she brought in her things. *Stupid! So stupid of me.*

The driver split off and headed toward the front door. Myers was the one who usually drove, and this man wasn't Myers. Through the wavy pane, Gwen could see him reach and pull a dark object from behind his back. She squinted and moved her head around so she could get a better view through the distorting glass. She couldn't be sure, but by the way he held it in front with two hands and pointed at the ground, it looked just like—*oh damn!* It was a gun.

"Shit, shit." *Where's the rifle? The bedroom.*

Had she locked the door leading from the kitchen to the garage? She couldn't remember.

Gwen turned to bolt for the bedroom, where she had sat the rifle down on the bed, intending to clean it before putting it back in the gun safe. She reconsidered, spun, and headed back down the hall to the kitchen. After racing to the door that separated the kitchen from the garage, she thumbed on the lock, a second before the knob rattled.

There was pounding on the front door, and then a sound like breaking glass. She reversed and took two steps back toward the bedroom and the rifle. Another crash told her the passenger was breaking through the hollow-core door between the kitchen and garage. She stood motionless like one of those damn deer caught in the headlights.

Crack! And Gwen felt something punch her upper arm. The man had fired his gun at her through the half-destroyed kitchen door. Another shot rang out, and drywall dust filled the air.

Heart pounding, Gwen raced out of the kitchen, past the front door, where a hand was snaking through the broken pane to turn the deadbolt, and down the hall toward her bedroom. A bathroom, spare bedroom, and her master bedroom led off the hall. On her way through, she slammed shut the doors of the spare room and bathroom. If all the doors were shut, they wouldn't know which one she had entered. The delay in having to check each room might give her a tiny advantage.

After tearing through her bedroom and shutting the door behind her, Gwen unlatched the window that opened to the backyard and tried to yank it up. It was stuck. She saw the window glass had blood on it. Hers.

Her mind flashed back to the garnet smear on Richard's sliding glass door. Her stomach lurched.

Gwen's right arm throbbed and she was clumsy with it. She looked at it and saw her sleeve was ripped and blood streamed.

She jerked again at the window. She heard the men's voices as they started down the hall. A doorknob rattled. The guest room.

A shuffle of feet on the hardwood floor, and then one of them said, "Not here."

Another doorknob rattled. Another door opened.

The bathroom.

Gwen was out of time.

Giving up on the window, and pulling the heavy drape across it to hide the blood, she grabbed the rifle off the bed and took it out of the case. She slid off the safety and sank down in the narrow space between the bed and the far wall. Gwen rested the rifle on top of the bed, aimed at the door, and then pulled a pillow over the top to hide the barrel and stock. She was right-handed, and the bullet had hit something that made it painful and clumsy. Could she shoot with her left?

"Missus Lindstrom, hey, we just need to talk to you. Sorry about the door. Just come on out." His tone changed from friendly to ominous. "Or it's going to be real bad if we have to come get you."

She had a brief thought about her phone, but it sat, what seemed like miles away, on the kitchen counter. *Crap.*

She was trembling so hard she worried about the quivering pillow on top of the rifle giving her away.

"Last chance," one of them said.

The cheerful way he said it, like he was offering an item on sale, made Gwen's stomach churn and bile rise in her throat. These men were evil, and they were looking forward to hurting her.

The knob turned, and Gwen heard the creak of the bedroom door slowly opening. She heard cloth rub against cloth as they moved, and smelled the musk of their adrenaline-induced excitement. Were they both inside her room now? She couldn't see anything behind the shelter of the pillow.

"I'm coming out. I'm coming out!" she cried. "Please don't shoot me."

She heard heavy breathing. Couldn't determine if it was her or all three of them.

Gwen raised a bloodied hand over the top of the pillow in surrender, sighted around the edge of it, and with her left hand, pulled the trigger.

The rifle boomed and kicked hard against her shoulder. She heard something heavy hit the floor.

"Fuck, fuck!" one of them shouted.

Gwen jerked the rifle from under the pillow. She ejected the shell and loaded another round, all the while sliding both her and the firearm under the high bed. Her arm hurt like hell.

Below the bottom of the comforter, she could see a dark figure writhing on the floor between her and the doorway. She was trapped.

She saw the shoes of the second man move around to the foot of the bed, and then she heard two rapid shots. The pillow that had fallen to the floor when she fired exploded, and foam stuffing rained down.

She took aim at the man's ankle nearest her and fired again. A shrill scream sounded, and a pistol clattered to the floor.

Gwen rolled out from under the bed, leaped over the still-moving first man, and sprinted down the hall. The blast of the gun in the tight space had ruined her hearing, and she felt more than heard her ragged panting.

On the race through the kitchen, Gwen grabbed the cell phone off the counter, bolted out the busted kitchen door, through the garage, and sprinted to the neighboring house. Crawling under an overgrown forsythia bush that hugged the fence, she punched out 911 with shaking and bloody fingers.

20

SAFE

"WHAT THE HELL WERE YOU THINKING?" VICKERS SNARLED.

The agents had arrived in Gwen's hospital room while she was in surgery to repair the wound in her arm. The wait for her to come out of the anesthesia and be taken to a room had not improved his mood.

In a calmer tone, Myers said, "Why didn't you just stay at the cabin?"

Jay, who had been sitting beside her hospital bed, held up a hand in a stop gesture.

"She tried to call but couldn't reach you."

"We had the phones off while we interviewed a witness at her lawyer's office," Vickers whined.

They most likely meant Katherine Saunders, but Gwen didn't say it.

"What about the two guys in my house," she croaked, her throat sore from the anesthesia.

"We're trying to identify them," Vickers said. "Neither had IDs on them. One man is recovering from surgery. Had to have his bowel repaired. The other isn't going to be walking for a while. You got him in the left ankle. We took their prints, and my guess is this wasn't their first rodeo. We'll figure it out."

"Nice shooting, by the way," Myers said.

"Yeah, I'll give you that," admitted Vickers.

A thought hit Gwen. "Are they here in the hospital?"

Vickers nodded. "Yes, but they're on a different floor, under guard, and handcuffed to the bed. Soon as they're out of danger, we'll transfer them to Cheyenne."

"I figured out what happened." Gwen tried to sit up, and Jay propped another pillow behind her back. "They, or the persons who hired them, were siphoning off money from the old Rhett Manufacturing pension accounts. Richard figured it out, and they must have realized they were in trouble."

She paused, reached for the water glass with her good arm. Jay handed it to her, adjusting the straw so she could drink.

Vickers and Myers traded a look.

Myers said, "That was our working theory. The interview with Saunders was helpful. There are still things to figure out— like who's behind it and where the funds ended up—but we'll get there. Meanwhile, Ms. Lindstrom, I want you to back away. Let us do our jobs. Understand?"

Not a problem. Gwen nodded her agreement.

She debated whether to give them what she had discovered or not, since they were shutting her out. She had already told them what she found. Just let them ask. Nicely.

"She's going to stay with me for a while," Jay told the investigators. "Keep us posted, okay?"

Staying with Jay for a while sounded good to Gwen. Until she could get repairs done, and the ghost of the attack exorcised, she didn't want to stay at home.

"Anything else?" She closed her eyes. "I'm very tired."

21

EPILOGUE

After three weeks, the doctor released Gwen to go back to work. She didn't tell him that she had already been at the restaurant, monitoring the staff and doing paperwork. She even gave her office a thorough decluttering, getting a strange satisfaction out of shredding outdated records.

As far as her stay with Jay, they took a two-day trip to the Tetons, and although Gwen still couldn't yet properly flip a fishing line into the water with her bum arm, they hiked and had meals at a couple great Jackson restaurants.

"I enjoyed this. Let's plan a time to escape for a vacation again," Jay had told Gwen, as she packed to move back into her repaired house.

"I'm going to hold you to that." She gave him a fierce hug.

The men who had attacked Gwen were in the Cheyenne jail, and the judge had ordered that they could not be bonded out. Gwen felt fairly safe. But still, one of the restaurant customers had installed monitoring systems with cameras and alarms at both the Ranchers Café and Gwen's house. She did her part, making sure the windows and doors were locked, even during the day, and watching to make sure no one followed her. That was easy since no one was usually on the streets as she traveled to work before dawn.

Vickers called Gwen after winter had stripped the leaves from the trees and coated the ground with white.

"The US Attorney for the District of Wyoming filed fraud and theft charges this morning," he said. "It took a while, but we were able to trace WON International and Matrix back to the principals."

"Who are they?" Gwen asked.

"There are three principals. Two are a husband and wife team living in Boca Raton. That's in Florida. The other is in New York. Most likely, they have mob connections, and we're still working on that angle. I suspect we'll find that this happened with other companies—ones that had once been family or independently owned. But right now, we're just charging on your assault and the Rhett case. That last, of course, isn't official, and you didn't get it from me."

Silence while Vickers considered what he had said.

"You need to keep all that to yourself."

"Not a problem," Gwen said, with a smile in her voice. "As long as they stay in Florida and New York, I'm done with my investigating."

"Good thing," Vickers snarled and hung up.

As far as Gabe's missing pension money, that might take a while to trace, Vickers had told her. But he didn't sound hopeful that she would ever see it.

"Sorry, honey. I tried," Gwen said heavenward.

There were still things to be thankful for: the bad guys were in jail, she had survived with only a scar to show for it, the repairs on her home were complete, and she and Jay had plans for a future vacation. In the meantime, she had a restaurant to run.

The End

Dear reader,

We hope you enjoyed reading *MAZE*. Please take a moment to leave a review, even if it's a short one. Your opinion is important to us.

Discover more books by Connie L. Beckett at
https://www.nextchapter.pub/authors/connie-l-beckett

Want to know when one of our books is free or discounted?
Join the newsletter at
http://eepurl.com/bqqB3H

Best regards,

Connie L. Beckett and the Next Chapter Team

ABOUT THE AUTHOR

Connie Beckett resides in northeast Kansas, where she is working on *Sweet Creek*, the third book in the Gwen Lindstrom series. In addition to the mystery series, Connie is the author of *Kingmaker and the Scribe.* Under the pen name Teter Keyes, she writes pre-teen fantasy novels, including *Lost Lamb: A Deidre Ann Adventure.*

In *Sweet Creek,* the next book in the Gwen Lindstrom Mystery series, Gwen Lindstrom and Jay Marker escape the Dubois winter to visit Jay's brother in Florence, Oregon. On a hike to scenic Sweet Creek Falls, they find a man's body bobbing against the edge of the pond.

To learn more about Connie and upcoming books, visit **www.-conniebeckett.net**

MAZE
ISBN: 978-4-82411-195-1

Published by
Next Chapter
1-60-20 Minami-Otsuka
170-0005 Toshima-Ku, Tokyo
+818035793528

6th November 2021

9 784824 111951